W9-AZU-777

If I don't leave now, one of these days my feelings for Jack will come out. I'll say or do something that will embarrass both of us.

Opening a new Word document, she began typing. "Dear Mr...." She paused. Gracie didn't call Jack "Mister." She started again. "Dear Jack: After five years, I think it's time I moved on to a new challenge...."

What new challenges? She'd loved every minute of her time at LIT. She'd been part of their team of three. They'd built the business from the ground up, an exciting experience, a privilege. Not one boring day in five years, more than she'd hoped for fresh out of business school. At twenty she'd interviewed for this job and fallen in love with Jack, all in the same day. Now she had to break away....

* * *

**Look for all these titles in
Lyn Cote's SISTERS OF THE HEART series:**

Books by Lyn Cote

Love Inspired

Never Alone #30
New Man in Town #66
Hope's Garden #111
Finally Home #137
Finally Found #162
The Preacher's Daughter #221
*His Saving Grace #247

*Sisters of the Heart

LYN COTE

now lives in Wisconsin with her husband, her real-life
hero. They raised a son and daughter together. Lyn has
spent her adult life as a schoolteacher, a full-time mom
and now a writer. Lyn's favorite food is watermelon.
Realizing that this delicacy is only available one season
out of the year, Lyn's friends keep up a constant flow
of "watermelon" gifts—candles, wood carvings, pillows, cloth bags, candy and on and on. Lyn also enjoys
crocheting and knitting, watching *Wheel of Fortune*
and doing lunch with friends. By the way, Lyn's last
name is pronounced "Coty."

Lyn enjoys hearing from readers. They can contact
her at P.O. Box 864, Woodruff, WI 54568 or by
e-mail at L.cote@juno.com.

HIS SAVING GRACE

LYN COTE

Published by Steeple Hill Books™

STEEPLE HILL BOOKS

Steeple
Hill®

ISBN 0-373-87257-7

HIS SAVING GRACE

Printed in U.S.A.

Parents, do not treat your children in such a way as to make them angry.

—*Ephesians* 6:4

To my wonderful friends, my fellow Love Inspired authors. You're a blessing in my life.

Prologue

He grinned, staring at the computer monitor, the only brightness in the dark room. Glee roared through him. He was invading files, data, territories not meant for him. Rows and rows and columns and columns of names, dates, diagnoses, procedures done, doctors and prescription names, cost, but primarily numbers.

His gaze fixed on the many zeros on the glowing screen. An angry voice deep in his memory replayed, *"That's all you'll ever be—a nothing. A zero."* His hand trembled as it hovered over his mouse, then he moved his cursor to a random column. He hadn't gone to all this trouble for nothing. He'd add a few zeros. That would make things interesting again.

Chapter One

Gracie Petrov had come to work this morning with a clear goal in mind: to resign. Ten hours later she was still circling it, unable to take the last fateful step and tell this to her boss, Jack Lassater. *Dear Father, everything in my mind tells me to do it—say it now. But my heart...* She felt a tightness over her heart. She pressed a hand there, trying to suppress the pain.

Why did I ever think Jack would notice me as a woman? I'm just his faithful girl Friday, an extension of his computer network.

The phone rang. She leaned over and picked up the receiver from her oak desk. Her greeting came out automatically: "LIT, Lassater Information Technology. This is Grace Petrov speaking. How may I help you?"

"Gracie, you're not home." Her father's voice scolded her in the kindest tone.

His concern brought a lump to her throat. She promised herself silently that her next job would definitely have regular hours. "I'm sorry, Dad. I—"

"I know. I know. You're trying to get the 'brain' to close up shop for the day."

Dad, it's more than that. "I won't be much longer." Speaking these words made her more aware of her fatigue. The inverted triangle of muscles across her shoulders, which created a V between her shoulder blades, ached from sitting in front of the computer for hours.

"I've heard *that* before. Okay. I'll make a plate of supper for you and put it in the fridge."

"Don't bother. Jack went out to get us a couple of hot dogs."

"That sounds healthy," he teased. "Just remember you're staying home tomorrow. It's Saturday. We have to give your cousin's room a fresh coat of paint. There's only a week before your cousin will be home."

She tried to put a smile into her voice. "Gotcha! 'Bye."

Her father just chuckled and hung up.

Gracie put the receiver in the cradle and stepped away from her desk. Looking out the tenth-story window, she glanced downward and glimpsed Jack. His straight back was toward her—broad shoulders in a tan knit shirt. His reddish brown hair shone in the golden twilight.

Oblivious to her as always, he had paused at the corner newsstand to talk to Old Louis as he shut down for the night. Everyone called the man Louis because his gravelly voice sounded just like that of the late Louis Armstrong. She leaned her head against the window. Jack always stopped to share a conversation with the toothless, elderly man. It was one of the things about Jack that had snared her heart.

But the flip side of this endearing trait puzzled his partner, Tom. Jack never spoke with their paying customers until *after* Tom had nailed down the deal. Then Jack only wanted to discuss the software project with the customer. There was no chatting or socializing, strictly business.

It frustrated Tom, but Gracie realized Jack wasn't merely a quiet man. Long before she'd ever met him, some part of him had shut down. She thought she knew why it had happened, but what could she do about it?

The phone rang again, and forgetting to let the machine pick up, she answered.

A man cleared his throat. "This is Dr. Cliff Lassater. Is Jack in?"

Dr. Lassater, Jack's father? Startled, Gracie drew in a deep breath. He had never called here before. In fact, she knew that Jack hadn't seen his father in…how long?

But she couldn't let her curiosity show. To a stranger like Dr. Lassater, she was just the executive assistant at LIT and should act like one. She kept her voice businesslike.

"I'm sorry, Dr. Lassater. Jack isn't here. May I take a message?"

"I know it's late. I thought I'd get your machine."

"I'm just getting ready to leave." The truth of this sentence hit her with sudden force. She pushed away the heavy feeling of finality.

"Well, then…I'm glad I caught you. I'd like to schedule a business lunch with Jack as soon as possible."

She would have told any other prospective client that Jack's partner handled customers. But maybe this time, Jack would talk to his father—as a client. She doubted it. She automatically asked him for a phone number, then realized she shouldn't have to ask for it. Surely Jack had it. Or did he?

Dr. Lassater didn't act surprised, and gave her his work and home numbers.

"Thank you, Doctor. I'll give Jack the message." As she hung up, she tried to come up with the reason for this unexpected contact. None came to mind, other than the obvious one. Dr. Lassater needed Jack's professional services. But was she correct? Something didn't feel right.

Her mind reverted to her own dilemma, trying to leave the man she loved. Her tender feelings for Jack were a one-way street, had been and would always be.

He was handsome, brilliant and an up-and-coming light in the information technology field. A real catch.

But so far neither she nor any other woman possessing more beauty and better credentials than she had broken through to him. His preoccupation with what fascinated him most—designing intricate programs for the medical field—was his impenetrable shield.

How much longer can I keep my feelings about Jack hidden? Why put off resigning any longer? The time had come to make the break. She'd write her letter of resignation and then go home for the night. When Tom returned from vacation, she'd give it to Jack. But she would write the letter now and have it ready.

Sighing, she turned away from the window and plunked down in front of her desk. *I can't face another mood-filled day like this. And if I don't leave now, one of these days my feelings for Jack will come out. I'll say or do something that will embarrass both of us.*

Opening a new document, she began typing. "Dear Mr...." She paused. She didn't call Jack "Mister." She deleted "Mr." and started again. "Dear Jack: After five years, I think it's time I moved on to a new challenge...."

What new challenge? She'd loved every minute of

her time at LIT. She'd been part of their team of three. Jack, Tom and she had built this business from the ground floor up, an exciting experience, a privilege.

Not a boring day in five years—more than she'd hoped for, fresh out of business school. At twenty, she'd interviewed for this job with LIT and fallen in love with Jack, all in the same day. Now she had to break away.

The door opened. Jack walked in.

Quickly, she set up a file to save her resignation letter under the name "Sassafras," a word her late mother had used to express frustration over something she couldn't get to work right.

Carrying two white paper sacks, Jack nodded and walked past her into his office. His lack of verbal greeting bothered some people. It made them think Jack was snubbing them. But she knew his mind was probably working on some intricate software problem.

Rising, she walked into Jack's office, now rich with the scent of hot dogs and onions. He'd left her proofreading a letter to a client while he'd gone out to pick them up two Chicago hot dogs with everything. Now, they'd eat. Tonight, she'd make herself finish the client letter and her letter of resignation.

Her stomach rumbled, the aroma of onions getting to her. "Jack?" No response. "Jack?" she persisted.

His clear blue eyes gazed up at her.

Bracing herself against his attractiveness, she lifted

an eyebrow at him. "So what did Louis have to say for himself?"

As he handed her the wax paper-wrapped hot dog slathered with mustard, celery salt, relish and onions, he let his face form a broad grin. "He says the Cubs won't make it to the Series, no matter what anyone says."

"Big news." She grinned back and just enjoyed standing there looking at him, having him look back at her. He always affected her this way, drawing her to him. She could almost forget the letter she'd just started, the decision she'd made. *Oh, dear Lord, how can I leave? But how can I stay?*

"Hey!" The outer door banged open. "What are you two still doing here? It's nearly eight."

"Yes, Tom, we're still here." An idea flashed into her mind, a way to get Jack to return his father's phone call. With Tom on vacation, she knew Jack would never pursue this lead. And something in Dr. Lassater's voice had prompted her to think the call had been an important one and maybe not just business.

Tom, dressed in jeans and a white knit polo shirt, breezed in. "What's up?"

She swung around. "We got a call. A customer wants to set up a business lunch—"

Tom waved his hand, cutting her off. "Then, you two are going to have to take care of it. I'm due at O'Hare and I'm not canceling this trip. I haven't had a vacation for nearly two years and I'm outta here."

Probably at a normal office, the executive assistant would keep her mouth shut. But this wasn't that kind of office—and what did she have to lose now anyway? A file marked ''Sassafras,'' lurking on her computer, tugged at her midsection, gave her a shot of urgency. Maybe she could get Jack and his father talking before she left.

To reproach Tom, she lifted her chin. ''You're still leaving, even though you realize that Jack's almost done with the St. Louis system—''

''Don't scold, Mother.'' Tom walked past her and dropped into a chair that angled toward both of them. ''I know I haven't brought in a big job, and we need one. But while I'm gone, our resident genius—'' he motioned broadly toward Jack ''—will keep busy doing a few little tasks I've lined up for him. Just think how refreshed I'll be after two weeks in San Francisco, the City by the Bay!''

Tom had the gift of gab, the main tool of a salesman. Gracie's father had said the first time he'd met Tom that ''the man's tongue runs on wheels.'' But now Gracie frowned. Tom was the one in the partnership who enticed, met and negotiated with clients. But he'd been distracted lately. What was going on beneath this loquacious man's surface? Something didn't click.

''Who called?'' Tom asked. ''Someone we've done business with before?''

Well, she'd brought it up. There was no going

back. She braced herself. "It was Jack's father, Dr. Lassater."

"What? What does he want?" Jack's face showed surprise and annoyance.

Tom leaned forward. "Hey, that's great news. Hope Medical Group's Board is one of the biggest in the city." Tom's tone changed. "Though I know Jack ignores that unimportant stuff. This could turn out to be a nice chunk of change."

Jack scowled.

Tom grinned. "You're the one who's been champing at the bit for more business."

"Not *his* business." Jack's jaw jutted out at a stubborn angle. "You're the negotiator. I'm the designer. It can wait till you get back."

"What's wrong with a little nepotism?" Tom teased and then shrugged. "Suit yourself. But if we lose it, don't blame me." With that, Tom rose, gathered up a few items from his desk and escaped.

Just the two of them again. Gracie gazed at Jack's profile. He'd turned on his monitor and opened a file. Did he do it to shut out Tom, or was he avoiding responding to the news of his father's call?

She didn't even try to catch Jack's attention. She'd guessed how he would react to his father's call and she'd given it her best shot.

Walking out, she closed the door behind her. LIT needed money, but Jack clearly wouldn't contact his father, not even as a customer. She'd been wrong to spring the news of Dr. Lassater's call in front of

Tom. When Dr. Lassater called again, she'd let him do his own persuading.

She sat by the window, chewing her juicy hot dog and worrying over what was going on with Tom. He definitely wasn't telling them something. *Why am I stewing over this? I'll be leaving soon.*

The phone rang and Gracie regarded it with a sinking heart. Jack's father wouldn't call back so soon, would he? Glancing at the clock, she pursed her lips. *Doesn't anyone know that offices should close at five?* "LIT—"

"Gracie, is…Jack…there?" Pain made itself heard in tiny gasps between words.

Gracie recognized Jack's mother's voice immediately. "What's wrong, Sandy?"

"I took…a…fall—"

"Where are you?" Gracie stood up. Sandy, who suffered from rheumatoid arthritis, had become her friend over the past five years.

"At the bottom of…my basement stairs. I…finally crawled over to …the wall phone…pulled it down."

"I'll get Jack. Are you bleeding?"

"No, I'm…just having…trouble breathing. Maybe I…cracked a rib."

Gracie started toward Jack's door. "Did you lose consciousness?"

"No. I'm just in a…lot of pain."

"We'll call 9-1-1 and be right over. Hang up and we'll call you back on Jack's cell phone." Grace hung up. "Jack!"

* * *

The cloying warmth and humidity of the summer night closed around Jack, but it didn't touch the chill snaking through him. He fumbled with the key at his mother's back door. *Come on. Come on.*

Beside him, Gracie spoke into his phone. "We're here, Sandy."

"Great. I'm really...feeling bad."

The lock released and Jack shoved open the door. "Mom!" He raced down the steep steps to the basement.

"Jack." His mother lay crumpled on the throw rug at the bottom of the stairs. Her face, so pale in the scant light, jolted him.

"I think...I need...to go to...the hospital—"

Her words were cut off by the sound of the siren. *Thank God.* Jack knelt beside her. "We called 9-1-1 on our way out of the office. The ambulance is really close."

"I'll go up and let them in." Gracie turned and ran back up the steps. "I can't believe they didn't beat us here."

"Where does it hurt?" Jack gently touched his mom's shoulder, angry with himself for not knowing what else to do for her.

"I may have cracked...some ribs." She paused, her breathing labored. "I can't...get up. I feel everything...but—"

Two EMTs charged down the steps. Jack fell back, giving them room in the area at the base of the stairs.

The men in uniform rattled off questions as they took her pulse and checked her limbs.

"Is it serious?" Jack asked.

"We'll get her to hospital for X-rays. You are her…?"

"Son."

They nodded. Soon the men had his mom on a rigid stretcher and were carrying her upstairs and out to the ambulance. He and Gracie got back in his small sedan and drove behind them to the hospital.

"I need to call my dad." Gracie opened his cell phone.

"You should have gone home. I shouldn't have let you come along."

"I couldn't have just gone home," she said with a sharpness in her voice he rarely heard. "I'd have been worried sick." She began talking into the phone, explaining to her dad what had happened.

Jack concentrated on following the red taillights of the ambulance. He tried to pray, but no words came to his worried mind. He'd known something like this was bound to happen sooner or later. He'd warned Mom about those stupid steps. But what good did that do now?

The arrival at the hospital made him crazy. Medical personnel pushed him aside and relegated him and Gracie to the hallway. He watched helplessly as his mom's gurney was pushed from one location to another.

* * *

"Jack, come here." Gracie took his arm, led him to a row of stiff plastic chairs and pushed him into one. She sat down beside him. He sprang up, unable to sit still.

His gaze lingering in the direction his mother had been taken, he said, "I'll call you a cab and send you home."

"No, I'll stay. I told you I couldn't just go home."

A tall distinguished-looking doctor hurried down the hall toward them. "Jack? Why is your mother here?"

Irritation zigzagged through Jack. "You're here? I didn't know this was one of your hospitals." He stared at his father and felt his jaw clench.

"I was called in on another emergency consult." His father studied him, but went on with emotion. "An ER staffer paged me, thinking I might be a relative of Sandy Lassater. What happened?"

Jack bristled, wanting to send his father away. He couldn't forget the past sins that lay between them. But he only said, "She fell down the basement stairs."

"Is she in X-ray?"

Jack nodded, pressing his lips together, holding back cutting words. Mom wouldn't want him arguing with his father here.

His dad frowned. "I'll go check on her."

Jack fumed in silence. What choice did he have? Maybe his father being a doctor would get his mother special attention, but the thought galled Jack.

His father glanced over at Grace. "This is…?"

"I'm Gracie, Dr. Lassater." She rose and offered him her hand. "I recognized your voice from your call earlier this evening."

Dr. Lassater shook her hand. "Right, the call. I do need to discuss business with LIT. But now I'll go see if I can help Sandy out."

The words grated on Jack. After all his father had done to hurt his mother, Jack wanted to snap, *We don't want you help.* But he couldn't. Mom just might need him. *Dear Lord, help her. I'm powerless here.*

Chapter Two

Much later, after Jack sent a reluctant Gracie home in a taxi, he drove his mother home. The June night's unusual heat and humidity hadn't abated—not even after midnight—and it added to his aggravation.

As soon as Jack climbed out of his air-conditioned car, sweat beaded his forehead. He hurried to the house and unlocked his mother's back door. Then he returned to the passenger side of the car.

"I still think they should have kept you overnight."

"I wasn't injured badly enough to be hospitalized." His mom turned on her seat and stiffly held her arms toward him. "I just took a fall. And you know how I feel about hospitals."

He didn't like the way she inhaled so carefully,

like every breath hurt her. "Two cracked ribs, a sprained right ankle and a chipped right kneecap—"

"—isn't serious enough for me to be kept overnight."

"I bet—" Jack assisted his slender mother to her feet and helped her prop herself against the open door "—if you were still Dr. Cliff Lassater's wife, they'd have insisted you stay overnight."

"Jack, you shouldn't be so bitter." She waited while he got her crutches out of the back seat and then she positioned them under her arms. "Your father didn't divorce me to hurt you."

Jack ignored her comment. "I can carry you—"

"I can walk with crutches. I'll just take it slow." She began to limp toward the back door, pausing after each step.

Jack slammed the car door, hit the automatic lock on the key ring and hurried ahead to hold the door open for her.

Inside, she insisted he let her "hop" up the three steps to the kitchen, holding on to the reinforced railing he'd put in two years ago. Then she limped through the kitchen to the front hall staircase and paused, panting.

That's enough. "Mom, it's late. I'm carrying you up to your bedroom."

She turned to him. "All right," she conceded in a pained, weakened voice, "but just this once. I have to be able to do this on my own—"

"Don't worry!" He couldn't keep the frustration out of his tone. "Tomorrow I'll make you go jogging with me!"

She chuckled and then froze as if that too pained her. "Jogging? *Now*—" she forced out each word, one by one "—you're…frightening…me."

He propped her crutches against the banister and then lifted her into his arms—a light burden. He climbed the worn stairs and deposited her on her bed. Then he hustled down for her crutches.

"Thank you, Jack." Sighing cautiously, she motioned him to rest the crutches on a chair beside her bed. "Now I'll be able to manage. You go home and get some sleep."

He'd already thought ahead to this moment. "I think I'll spend the night in my old room—"

"Jack—"

"It's late, and it will give me more time to sleep," he alibied with a straight face.

His mom shook her head at him. "All right. I'm too tired to argue with you. And you're always welcome here anyway."

He looked around her small bedroom. He couldn't stop himself. "I wish you'd let me help you buy something newer—a ranch-style with everything on one level and larger—"

"Not that again!" she scolded. "I like this house. I love this neighborhood where I know everyone and—"

"—and it has a corner store and a rapid transit station within walking distance." He recited the litany of reasons she'd given over the years for not moving.

"Exactly. If I'd wanted to move, I would have. I didn't and I don't."

"But those basement steps—"

"Don't fuss over me!" Irritation finally leaked into her tone. "Go get some sleep. I'll be fine. This isn't my first time using crutches." In spite of her brave words, she was wilting visibly. She drew in a shallow breath. "I know what I'm doing."

Sorry he'd provoked this outburst, he held up both hands in surrender. "Okay, good night, Mom." He bent and kissed her cheek.

She patted his. "I'll see you in the morning."

"Okay." He made himself walk across the hall to his old bedroom. The air-conditioning at the hospital had been much more effective than his mom's old unit. Breathing in the stuffy air of the unused bedroom, he switched on a box fan on the floor. Then he flung back the navy-blue comforter on the twin bed he'd slept on in high school. Kicking off his shoes and shrugging out of his knit shirt and slacks, he flopped down on the bed.

His body ached. But it wasn't waiting at the hospital on uncomfortable plastic chairs that had knotted his neck muscles. *What's going on? I don't see my*

*father for how long? And then in one evening, he
calls and I run into him at the hospital?*

Jack turned over onto his stomach. Seeing his dad
stirred up thoughts he rarely allowed to intrude—like
his dad's trophy wife, a very young red-haired trophy
wife. Or rather, ex-trophy wife.

Feelings buzzed around inside him like angry bees.
He closed his eyes, concentrating on the soothing
whir of the fan and its cooling breeze drifting over
him. But his mind refused to be lulled to sleep.

"I need to discuss business with LIT"—that's
what his father had said. "Well, I'm not the only
game in town, *Dad*," Jack grumbled sideways into
his pillow. "You're not going to draw me into your
life again with this lame ploy."

Once again, an image of his father driving out of
the hospital parking lot in his new Mercedes came
to mind. *It isn't fair, Lord. Mom should have what
she needs. He has so much and she has so little. It
isn't fair.*

But Jack would make up the difference. His
mother would never want for anything if he could
help it—and fortunately, he could.

At the chrome red and white kitchen table around
ten o'clock the next morning, Gracie sipped her
dad's strong morning coffee. She was wearing faded
cutoffs and a tattered white T-shirt—her painting
clothes. The outfit suited her grumpy and "at odds"

mood. Her dad, Mike Petrov—lean and wiry with salt-and-pepper hair—was similarly dressed in a spattered khaki work shirt and jeans. He looked relaxed, but why was he eyeing her so strangely?

"You shouldn't have let me sleep in," Gracie complained, while swallowing a self-incriminating yawn. "I wanted to get this painting started early so we're done before the afternoon heat."

"You didn't get in until long after midnight," her dad explained in his easygoing voice, ignoring her crankiness.

These words stated so calmly alerted Gracie. "Okay. What do you want to know, Dad?"

He grinned at her. "Why did you stay so late at the hospital with your boss? You could have come home."

Gracie sipped her coffee, hiding her mouth behind her cup. Jack was the last person she wanted to talk about. She pictured Jack waiting with her for a taxi at the curb in front of the hospital. Jack was a maddening mix of unexpected solicitude and vague neglect. Gracie took a bite of buttery blackberry-jammed toast.

"So, what's going on with you and Mr. Brain Lassater?"

"Going on?" Suddenly, her recurring daydream of Jack sweeping her into his arms flitted through her unruly mind. She felt her cheeks warm. "Nothing's going on." She pleated the soft, well-worn cotton tablecloth between her fingers. *Thanks to Jack, nothing is going on, and apparently it never will.*

Childish footsteps pounded down the back staircase of the two-flat. The back door flew open, banging the wall behind it.

Gracie flinched, then smiled.

Her twin four-year-old nephews—Austin and Andy—threw themselves at her. "Aunt Gracie! Aunt Gracie! We get to help you and Grampa paint this morning!"

"What?" Though glad of the interruption, Gracie held her coffee mug high above their boisterous hugs. Then she turned a quizzical expression to her dad sitting across from her. "Nobody told me."

Her dad shrugged. "Don't look at me."

"I hope you won't mind." Annie, Gracie's younger sister, petite and dark-haired just like Gracie, stood apart from them in the kitchen door. "Troy has to work today at the job site and I need to take care of…some things."

Annie sounded funny, as if she were covering up for something. Gracie scrutinized her sister. Did these "things" have anything to do with the raised voices over the past few weeks and doors slamming upstairs very late last night? Gracie swallowed that question, recalling the first law of living near relatives—don't pry.

Annie avoided Gracie's eyes. "I won't be gone long." Then she glanced at her sister.

Gracie stilled at the defiant look in Annie's eyes. "But—"

"Gotta go!" Annie backed toward the door. "I can't change plans now." She paused at the door and then came back. She hugged each of her blond, blue-eyed sons, miniatures of their father, and kissed them. "Be good until Mommy comes back, okay?"

"Okay!" the boys chorused.

Then Annie escaped out the door.

Gracie and her dad exchanged glances. Hers asked, *What's with Annie, and how are we going to paint a room with the* help *of two four-year-old boys?*

His unspoken reply: *I don't have a clue. I guess we'll manage.*

"Okay, boys," her dad said, "let's strip you down to your briefs. We're moving everything out of cousin Patience's room so we can paint it for her before she comes home next week." Her dad yanked off the boys' shirts and shorts, tossing them on a kitchen chair.

In Spider-Man briefs, the twins danced around them, chanting, "Will we really get to paint? Huh? Really? Huh?"

Gracie nodded. Still, the defiant expression on her sister's face kept coming back to her.

God, speak to Annie today. Make her aware of how blessed she is with a loving husband and two adorable boys. Please!

* * *

Around ten on Saturday, the morning after the rush to the hospital, Jack rolled over, yawning. Then he was awake, looking up at the ceiling in his old room at Mom's and then over at the bedside clock. He sat up and rubbed his face with his hands. Before he could give in to temptation and roll back over to sleep, he stood up and pulled on his slacks.

"Mom!" he called as he opened his door and looked across the hall.

His mom's bed was already neatly made. She was not in her room.

"Mom!" He shuffled down the stairs at a fast clip. "You should have got me up! You shouldn't have gone downstairs by yourself! What if you'd fallen?"

At the bottom of the staircase, he listened for her. He heard nothing. "Mom!" He headed toward the kitchen. *She wouldn't go back down those basement steps again, would she?* Worry picked up his pace.

After passing through the kitchen, he flipped on the light switch in the basement stairwell and listened for movement below. Then he heard his mom's voice—outside. She shouldn't be hopping up and down, in and out!

Jack jerked open the back door and leaned out. The heat from the asphalt drive wafted up into his face. The large round thermometer on the garage already read ninety-two degrees Fahrenheit. At the fence on the other side of the driveway, his mom was talking to her next-door neighbor.

"Mom?"

Leaning on her crutches, Sandy turned back. "Finally woke up?"

"Hey!" Mr. Pulaski, the grizzled retired police sergeant who lived next door, greeted him. "How're ya doin', Jack? Invented anything lately?"

Jack swallowed the lecture about being more careful that he'd intended to give his mother. Instead, he waved at Mr. Pulaski, who had no sons or grandsons and who had come to all of Jack's high school football games. "Nothing special."

"I'll come in and make you some breakfast." Using her crutches, Sandy began her slow limping toward Jack.

"I told yer ma she should do her laundry at the Laundromat. Then she wouldn't have to go down those stairs. They ain't safe for a lady who's got the arthritis so bad. If it weren't for this bum leg, I'd take it for her."

"I'm with you a hundred percent. And don't worry. I'll take care of it." Jack ushered his mother inside and closed the door behind them. *"Mom—"*

"Now, don't fuss, Jack. I'm a little sore this morning, but my pain pills are doing their job, okay?"

He tamped down the string of cautions he had prepared. *She won't listen to me anyway.* "If you say so. Now sit down while I get myself some break-fast.''

She lowered herself with care into one of the kitchen chairs at the round oak table.

From the cupboard, Jack got a box of cereal, and from the fridge, a half gallon of milk, and he set them both down on the table. ''Mom, I was thinking. Why don't you move into my apartment until you're off crutches?''

''No, I want to be in my own home.''

''But, Mom, with the only bath upstairs, you have to go up and down stairs all day—''

''I'm staying right here.''

''Mom, why not take it easy for just a day—''

''No, dear, I'm fine right here.''

He frowned. ''You don't make this easy—''

There was a knock at the back door. It opened before either of them could answer it. ''Sandy? It's me, Cliff.''

His dad had nerve. Jack nearly growled, *Go ahead, just walk right in like you still own it, Doctor.*

Sandy shook her head at Jack. ''Come on in, Cliff.''

He hated the way people always catered to his dad, the *doctor.* Watching his dad out of the corner of his eye, Jack kept busy pouring cereal into his bowl and adding milk and sugar.

Cliff walked into the kitchen. From his dad's crisp

tan chinos and blue knit short-sleeved shirt, Jack surmised that he was on his way to play golf.

"I can't stay long, Sandy. I'm on my way to the links. I just wanted to see how you were doing this morning."

Jack kept his focus on his breakfast.

"I'm a little more achy than usual, Cliff," his mom replied. "But I'm going to be okay. I'm sure Jack will hover over me for the rest of the weekend."

Jack felt his father's attention on him. Warm in the face, he refused to look up.

"I was hoping you'd be here, son. I really need to make a date to talk with you about business—stat."

So, that's why you came here. Maybe you think Mom will pressure me for you? Jack glanced up. "My partner, Tom, who negotiates all our deals, is gone on a two-week vacation. I'll have him get back to you when he returns."

His dad frowned. "This can't wait that long."

Jack shrugged.

"Jack," his mom coaxed.

"Okay," Jack said to placate her, "call me again Monday morning."

"Great. I've got to go." His dad glanced at the gold Rolex on his wrist. "I'm golfing at the club today with two city aldermen and the chief surgeon from Northwestern Hospital. Sandy, call me if your condition worsens, okay?"

"Okay. 'Bye, Cliff." She waved.

The door closed and he was gone.

Jack sucked in acid words, his usual reaction to his dad. *Two city aldermen and a chief surgeon—we are impressed, Dad.* Jack chewed his crunchy wheat cereal as though chewing out his dad. Pretense. All show. And this visit was all about what his dad needed, not his mother's condition.

His mother cocked her head toward him. "What's this about Cliff wanting LIT to do a job for him?"

He didn't answer her.

"Your father's money spends just like any other," Sandy said with a rueful smile.

Jack didn't reply.

"Jack, your father and I've been divorced for years now. I've forgiven him. It's time you made peace with him and went on with your life."

"I am going on with my life. There's nothing wrong with my life."

His mom shook her head. "Son, holding in anger will only make *you* miserable. 'Forgive us as we forgive others,' remember?"

Later that day, long after lunch and the second coat of paint, the scent of latex hung in the stuffy air that wrapped around Gracie. She shuffled down the back steps to the cooler, shadowy basement laundry room and plopped the paint trays, brushes and rollers into the oversize laundry sink.

She swiped the perspiration off her face with the

hem of her damp T-shirt and then started running cool water over the first brush, riffling the bristles with her fingers, working out the paint. *Where are you, Annie? Why aren't you home yet?*

As if in reply, she heard the back door open and footsteps running up the rear staircase to the apartment upstairs. They sounded too heavy to be Annie's, but why would Troy be home this early in the afternoon? Usually when he had to work Saturdays, he worked late.

She concentrated on cleaning the brushes under the faucet. *I should call Sandy and see how she's doing today. But Jack's probably there.*

Thoughts from yesterday bombarded Gracie. Jack's image wouldn't give in and vanish. She worked harder on the brushes, trying to blot Jack from her mind and idly listening to the squeals of the twins as their granddad sprayed them with cold water outside in the backyard. It was cooler in the basement, but Gracie thought she just might go outside herself and get a refreshing spray—

Footsteps stormed down the back steps. "Gracie!" Troy, her brother-in-law, roared. "Gracie!"

The outrage in his voice jolted her. She dropped the roller and raced up the basement stairs. She met Troy at the top. "What is it?"

"I found this—" Troy's voice shook as he pushed a sheet of Annie's stationery at her.

Gracie took the page and looked down. She read the brief note once, twice. "I can't believe it!"

* * *

On Monday morning, at his desk, Jack tried Gracie's number one more time. Busy. Still busy. He'd come in to work, intending to find Tom's itinerary with Gracie's help. Instead, he'd found an empty office and only a brief message from Gracie on his answering machine: "Jack, I'm sorry I won't be in today. Family emergency."

What did that mean? Gracie never took personal days. She lived with her dad, a widower, and her sister and her family lived upstairs, he recalled vaguely.

"Gracie, I need you today," Jack complained to the empty office.

The office phone rang. Jack let the answering machine pick up. He waited.

"Hi, this is Cliff Lassater again. I need to set up a lunch appointment for this week. This situation can't be put on hold. Jack, please call me back ASAP." His dad's tone had sharpened several notches since Saturday.

Ignoring the unwelcome message, Jack glanced around the office that he'd already sorted through twice looking for Tom's vacation itinerary. If he didn't get busy with another project, his mother would "guilt" him into doing this job for his dad.

He didn't trust his dad's motives. He couldn't. But

his mom had already mentioned her hope that he
would help out his father. "Jack, why don't you
show your father what you can do?" she'd asked.
"Be big about it."

"I'm not interested in impressing my father," Jack
said now, under his breath.

In a burst of frustration, he headed out, snapping
the lock on the LIT door behind him. In his pocket,
he had Gracie's home address. He'd find out what
was keeping her away from the office and tying up
the phone all morning. *Is everything going haywire?*

After an aggravatingly slow traffic-filled drive
from downtown to a north-side neighborhood, he
pulled over and parked in front of the white vinyl-
sided two-flat. After checking Gracie's address again,
he climbed out. He locked the car, opened the chain-
link gate and walked up to the glossy kelly-green
front door. He pressed the doorbell, heard it trilling
inside and waited. Now that he'd arrived, uncertainty
gripped him. What had kept Gracie home? Maybe he
should mind his own business.

To get his bearings, he glanced around at the older
neighborhood of neat two-flats and a few single-
family Victorian houses. At the corner started a
block-long commercial area with a local grocer, a
drugstore, a laundry and dry cleaner, an obviously
ethnic Polska Café, and across the street from the
stores, a large redbrick church, St. Wenceslas.

Through the windowed door, he eyed the roomy

foyer that had three doors—one directly opposite him to the flight of stairs to the second story, one to his right to an enclosed porch, and just behind that one, a door that led traditionally to the first-floor apartment.

That door opened. Gracie looked out at him. "Jack?"

Her shocked tone made him feel awkward. He'd never before invaded Gracie's private life. "I'm sorry, but I need some information—" He stopped.

Gracie didn't look like herself at all. Her short dark wavy hair was uncombed and she had dark circles under her eyes. And her blouse was wrinkled as though she'd slept in it.

"What's wrong with you?"

Gracie gaped at him. "What are you doing here?"

"Aunt Gracie, Aunt Gracie!" Children's voices came from inside. "Who's here?"

Sighing, Gracie turned and motioned Jack to follow her into the first-floor flat. "This is my boss, Mr. Lassater. Jack, these are my nephews, Austin and Andy."

After nodding at the boys, he scanned the room, which looked comfortable rather than designer-magazine fashionable. He liked the bright colors—yellow, blue and white.

"Boys," Gracie said, "you can go back outside—"

"No, we don't wanna," Andy whined. Both boys latched on to her arms.

"Okay, then," Gracie soothed. "How about I put on a video?"

The two little boys stared up at her.

"Come on, guys," Gracie coaxed them. "I'll put it in for you and then Jack and I will just be in the kitchen. He probably wants me to help him with something about work."

"You're not *goin'* to work today, are ya?" Andy asked, sounding worried.

"No, I told you I'm staying here with you. I won't leave. Don't worry." Gracie looked to Jack and indicated a doorway at the far end of the large living-dining room. "Go through there and have a seat at the kitchen table, Jack. I'll be right with you."

Jack did what he was told. But he didn't like the feeling of "bad news coming" that he was getting.

Chapter Three

Exhausted from a very restless sleep, Gracie plopped down in the chair across from Jack in the red and white kitchen. Her shoulders ached from lifting the twins, rolling on paint. From tension. She had plenty of that.

"What's wrong? Is it about business, or your mother?"

"What's wrong here?" Jack countered. "You look awful."

Gracie's eyes widened. "I *must* look awful if you noticed it. But I asked you first."

He propped one elbow on the table. He covered the lower half of his handsome face with his hand, a gesture she'd come to know, one she would miss when she left. *Still hiding, Jack?*

Happy cartoon voices floated in from the living

room. Leaning back, she waited. *Why did I try to hurry him? Jack thinks only in numbers, integers, logarithms, and about kludges and crackers.* She shut her scratchy, warm eyes.

She knew she should just go ahead and quit. She couldn't believe this was happening. What had gotten into Annie? *Dear God, please, what are we going to do?*

"What's got you all upset?" Jack asked.

Gracie stared down at her hands and saw that her knuckles were white. "My kid sister, Annie, has left her husband." As she voiced these words, anger sizzled through her.

"Your sister left her kids?" His tone condemned Annie.

Gracie felt her temper flare. "This isn't all Annie's fault. She's just so young."

Even though the cheery music from the video played on, without warning, the twins appeared in the doorway. Gracie looked into their down-turned faces.

"What is it, guys?"

"When's Mommy coming home?" Austin whined.

"Don't worry. Your mommy will be back before you know it."

Her nephews stared at her, looking unconvinced, and then wandered back to the video. Two little lost souls.

Dear Lord, put Your arms around them. I don't know how to keep this from wounding them deeply.

And then she wondered angrily, *Annie, what were you thinking?*

"Please, we have to be careful what we say in front of the twins," she said in a quiet voice. "I want to minimize the effect of this on them."

"Sorry." He'd lowered his voice, too. "How long have your sister and her husband been having problems?"

"They weren't having problems," Gracie snapped.

"Then, why did she leave?" Jack looked puzzled.

Gracie frowned and stared at the tabletop.

Gracie's expression and her hesitance told Jack that she didn't like talking about her sister in this way. "Better just tell me, Gracie," Jack said.

She looked at him then, a tear in one eye.

Oh, Gracie. Concern for her welled up inside him, warming him, surprising him with its force.

"My sister is really smart. She won all kinds of scholarships. We were so proud," Gracie admitted, then paused. "But she decided to marry right after high school."

Jack nodded, encouraging her to go on.

"She'd planned to go to college anyway. But she had the twins right away and then decided to postpone getting a degree until they were old enough for preschool—"

"You mean, about now?"

She pursed her lips. "Yes, but now, her husband, Troy, wants her to have another baby, finish their family, and then go to college when all three are in school."

"Sounds like he reneged on their deal." The same thing had happened to his mom. His dad had reneged on their deal. *Why was that so common?*

"Yes, but Annie shouldn't just leave," Gracie insisted. "She should stay and work it out with her husband."

Jack nodded. "Yes, but—"

The twins appeared beside them. "Video's over," one announced, and climbed into Gracie's lap.

When the other little guy climbed up on Jack uninvited, he was surprised. Jack couldn't remember ever having a small child in his lap. It was a strange feeling. Jack clamped an arm around the kid's middle, securing him in place.

The kid put small hands on Jack's arm, and across from Jack, his brother's expression was pinched. The urge to protect these little ones claimed Jack. *Poor kids.* Jack suddenly recalled Mr. Pulaski calling him over to rake leaves the day his dad had packed up and left home.

Jack shoved his chair back, nearly upsetting it. But he set the boy on his feet with care. "How about we walk Andy and Austin to that grocery store down the block? You guys can each pick out a candy bar." Jack stood there, surprised at himself.

Obviously tempted by this bribe, the twins wa-

vered. "Can we get one for our mommy?" one bar-
gained.

"And Aunt Gracie?" the other added.

"Sure—" Jack heard himself say. "A king-size
one for Aunt…Gracie, one for each of you, and one
for everyone else in your family."

Gracie flashed him a startled look. But she smiled,
too.

He felt blessed by it. With a nod to her, Jack
moved forward and shepherded the boys ahead of
him.

The kitchen phone rang and Gracie stopped to get
it.

Jack waited in the living room with the boys, who
held on to his hands and twisted them back and forth.

Standing in the doorway, Gracie made a face and
covered the receiver with her hand. "It's Annie's
mother-in-law. Can you go ahead and I'll catch up
with you?"

"Sure," Jack said with bravado, "I think I can
handle buying candy bars."

"Boys, be sure to hold Jack's hands when you
cross the street!" Gracie called after them.

Jack let the boys lead him down the front steps.
The sensation of such small hands in his again reinforced the desire to protect these little ones.

"Do we really get king-size ones?" one of the
twins asked, giving him a questioning look.

"Which one are you?" Jack asked, trying to get
his bearings.

"I'm Austin. I got a mole on my ear." The kid pointed to a small brown spot on his earlobe.

"And I don't got one. So you know I'm Andy." The other twin pointed to his naked earlobe.

"Okay. I got it. Austin has the mole. Andy is mole-less. And yes, you can get king-size ones."

They bobbed their heads up and down like puppets.

Realizing he was nearly dragging the boys along, Jack shortened his stride and then stopped at the corner.

Austin hung on Jack's hand, tugging and stretching as far as he could away from Jack. "Aunt Gracie works for you?"

"That's right." Jack watched at the corner for a break in traffic.

"You are real smart. Grampa says so." Andy imitated his brother, pulling on Jack's other arm.

Feeling like a tent with the twins as the pegs, Jack ignored this comment. "Come on. It's clear."

Clear, Lord, that I thought I had a problem. But these little guys are the ones who need Your help. They shouldn't suffer because their mom has left them. It's not right.

Later, after the king-size candy bar run and an hour after a grilled-cheese sandwich lunch, Gracie brought the twins out into the backyard. Still at her heels, Jack hadn't mentioned leaving, and, weakened by Annie's desertion, she'd let him stay. *I should*

have told him to go. I should just turn in my resig-
nation. But she couldn't. *This is just all too much,*
Lord.

Jack made a *whoosh* sound as he thrust each twin's
swing forward in turn. The boys squealed and kicked
their feet. "Higher! Higher!"

Gracie realized that Jack—who usually didn't appear aware of humans around him—had helped her
today in distracting the twins from the disappearance
of their mother. His unforeseen thoughtfulness
choked her up and lowered her mood even more.
*Why does Jack have to be so sweet when I'm going
to quit?*

"I should go now." Jack turned to her as if he'd
overheard her thoughts. "I need to check the answering machine at the office in case some client has
called with a problem."

"It's time for these guys to take a nap anyway,"
she said, ignoring the droop in her spirits. With Jack
here, she hadn't felt so turned upside-down. *I'm all
mixed up today, Lord. I want him gone, I want him
here.*

"I don't wanna nap," Austin complained.

"Me neither," Andy agreed. "We're not babies."

"I'll put on your favorite video and you can just
lie on our couch," Gracie said. "After you rest for
an hour, I'll take you to the park. Okay?"

"Yay!" the twins yelled in unison, and practically
jumped from the flying swings.

Soon the boys were lying on the couch, breathing

evenly. Gracie insisted Jack finish his iced tea from lunch before he left. Another confused delay tactic.

From the refrigerator, she handed him the chilled half-filled glass. In the distance, a church carillon marked time with a melody and chimed the hour, three p.m. A cartoon voice sang softly in the living room again. The seat of the kitchen chair felt hard under her. Every sensation swelled, seeming magnified. With her forefinger, she traced a bead of moisture on the outside of her frosty glass of tea.

Jack felt like he'd been trapped in a time warp. Today hadn't gone anything like he'd expected.

"I'm sorry to have taken up your time," Gracie said.

"That doesn't matter," he muttered. *My mom matters. What's happening here matters.*

Gracie looked into his eyes. "I've never heard you say *that* before." She paused. "You never told me why you came."

Gracie leaned toward him—or had he leaned toward her? What could he say? *I wanted to be too busy to do that job for my dad* sounded too weird. He drained his glass and stood up. "It was nothing. I'd better go."

"I'll walk you to your car," Gracie said, standing also.

He followed her through the living room, where the twins already slumbered. Their faces had relaxed in sleep, looking trouble-free yet more vulnerable. Jack took a deep breath as he slowed and glanced at

Gracie. She gave her nephews a loving glance filled
with concern.

A sudden and unreasoning twinge of jealousy
pinched Jack. Maybe being with Gracie's family had
just highlighted that he had only his mom.

Outside, Jack paused beside Gracie. They stood
near his car, stiff and unspeaking. Cars rushed up and
down the street.

He knew he should get in his sedan and leave, but
Gracie needed him. Gracie, who was always so organized and prepared for anything. He shoved his
hands into his pockets so he wouldn't give in and
reach out to touch her.

"You take off the next few days, whatever you
need."

She hesitated, visibly considering his offer.
"Thanks." She took a deep breath. "You should talk
to your dad," she urged. "His job might be something ridiculously easy for you to do while Tom's
gone. And money's money, Jack."

That's what his mom had said. He leaned against
a tree and looked into her eyes. *Gracie has gray eyes,
nice ones.* Had he noticed that before?

"Call him, Jack," Gracie murmured.

"I don't hear from him for years," Jack fumed,
"and now he calls my office and I meet him at the
hospital Friday, and he stops over at my mom's Saturday. This morning he calls my office again."

"Maybe you're reading too much into it. Maybe
he just wants you to do a job for him because you're

the best at what he needs done." Her voice was earnest.

He resisted the new and powerful attraction he'd felt for her all this unusual day. "With Tom on vacation and you on family leave—"

"Just call him back and set up a lunch date." She took a step closer. "What's so hard about that?"

"Having lunch with my dad tops my list of Things I Don't Want to Do." He folded his arms.

"How about if I went with you to that lunch? I can do that much." She waved to someone across the street. "A neighbor could watch the twins."

"No," he objected. "I wouldn't ask you to take time away from your family. The twins need you."

He turned away slightly, but still gazed at Gracie, wishing there was something he could do to ease her worry. But there wasn't anything more he could do for her or her nephews. And...why hadn't he ever noticed that she had a small mole on one of her ears?

"Well, you could always ask him to meet us—all of us—at the Polska Café." A shadow of a grin passed over Gracie's face. "I'm sure it's just his kind of restaurant."

Jack looked down the street at the busy neighborhood café. His dad with his Rolex and Brooks Brothers suit at the Polska Café? He chuckled. "Why not?"

"Jack, no. I was only joking."

"Then, the joke's on him." Jack chuckled and got into the car, ignoring Gracie's further objections.

* * *

The next day, Tuesday around noon, Gracie entered the Polska Café. She glanced around to make sure neither Jack nor his dad had already arrived for their business lunch. The little café, not redecorated since it opened in 1947, hummed with voices, laughter and the clatter of dishes and flatware. Gracie winced inside at the contrast between her worried self and the happy, unconcerned mood in the café.

"Hey! Gracie, how are you?" Plump, aproned Mama Kalanovski, standing behind the counter, leaned over to Gracie. "Any word from Annie?"

"She and Troy are talking...."

Ma clucked her tongue sympathetically.

Every day, the fact of Annie's leaving became harder to accept, not easier. And now, this business lunch. Gracie felt keyed up and dragged down at the same time.

"I need a table for three."

"Okay." Within moments, Mama had a table wiped and set. "Your dad and Troy coming?" Mama asked.

"No, my boss and his, uh...client." Gracie sat down, facing the entrance.

"Your big boss from downtown?" Mama's awed voice boomed over the jovial din. "The one Mike calls 'The Brain'?"

Nearby customers turned to look at Gracie. Not meeting anyone's eye, she nodded to Mama. *If Jack and his dad don't back out.*

Just then, Jack strode in, looking out of place in his business casual. The summer sunshine pouring through the front window lit up the red in his chestnut hair.

A brief break in the surrounding chatter alerted Gracie that his entrance had been duly noted. She waved, ignoring the attention Jack's entrance had drawn. Why did he have to look so good? *I have to resign…soon.* But Annie's leaving Troy had greatly overshadowed Gracie's dilemma over leaving Jack.

Gracie's love for Jack still simmered inside her, overlaid with hopelessness. She tightened her self-control, making her face blandly welcome.

Jack reached her. "Gracie, something's come up. Has Tom called you?"

"Tom?" Her face twisted in surprise. "No. Was he supposed to? What's happened?"

Jack sat down across from her. "He called me this morning on my cell phone. He said a few words, then we were cut off." Jack shrugged. "I tried to call him back but I couldn't get him."

"What did he want?" She recalled her own uneasiness about Tom the last time she'd seen him. So much had happened since that Friday evening. It felt like a thousand years ago.

Jack frowned. "What he said didn't make a lot of sense—"

"Is that your father?" Gracie cut in. She nodded toward the front. Jack rose. Gracie noted the hardening of his jaw as he motioned to the man who hesitated just inside the entrance.

Lord, I'm here to help Jack, to run interference between the two of them. Help me. I'm not up to this today.

Cliff Lassater, wearing a crisp, lightweight tan business suit, stood out like an alien. Most diners were retirees and workmen from nearby factories. He glanced around critically as he moved to join their table. Those around him returned his obvious inspection with a variety of reactions—lifted eyebrows, grunts and some glares.

Gracie sighed inwardly. She would be interrogated in the friendliest way for the next few weeks: *"Who was that with you at the Polska?"*

"Hello." Cliff greeted them. "You're Gracie, right?"

Gracie nodded.

After glancing at the chair as though assessing its cleanliness, Cliff sat down beside Jack. "Do you eat here often?" He asked the question in a tone that also asked, *Why would you eat in a place like this and why would you ask me to join you?*

Gracie bristled at the condescension in his tone. "I know this isn't what you're used to—"

"We can do business here." Jack leaned back in his chair. "That's what you wanted, isn't it?" His tone was a challenge to his dad.

"Well, I'm glad we're finally meeting." Cliff glanced around, looking increasingly uncomfortable.

"It's a bit crowded here. I'd hoped for a more confidential meeting place—"

"I don't think you have to worry—" Jack dismissed his father's objection with a wave "—about anyone here being interested in whatever problem you've come to discuss." He opened up his plastic-covered handwritten menu, closing the discussion.

Gracie smiled to soften Jack's abruptness. "The Polska is noted for its Polish and Slovenian specialties. They make all their sausage, baked goods and breads—everything from scratch."

Mama bustled over and distributed glasses of ice water. "Welcome to the Polska! Do you need more time, or do you know what you want?"

Cliff looked to Gracie instead of the menu. "Perhaps you could suggest something?"

"I'm going to have the spring salad and a poppy-seed roll," Gracie said. "In this heat, I can't eat much." That would be as good an excuse as any for her lack of appetite.

Mama clucked her tongue. "Okay, the spring and a poppy-seed for you. That's good, all right, but not enough for a bird."

"Well, I'll be a bird, too, then," Cliff said, and smiled. "Same for me."

Jack glanced at Mama. "I'll have your Reuben sandwich and iced tea."

"Very good." Mama beamed at him. "We make our own sauerkraut and rye bread." She bustled away.

"Jack, how is your mother?" Cliff asked, sounding to Gracie more polite than concerned.

"She's feeling better." Jack wouldn't look at his dad.

Gracie sensed the instant wall Jack had put up between him and his father. Did Cliff sense it, too?

"Why don't we get started with business?" Gracie suggested.

"Hope Medical has an untarnished reputation—" Cliff began.

"Cut to the chase," Jack interrupted in a brusque tone. "What is it that Hope Medical needs?"

Cliff grimaced and then cleared his throat. "Hope Medical Group is responsible for a few hospitals, clinical labs and several large practices in the metro area in a combined financial and medical organization." Cliff folded his hands on the table and leaned on his elbows. "We save money on financial costs by joining together. Somehow, our billing system has been compromised—"

"A hacker?" Jack asked.

"We don't know." Cliff looked even more uneasy. "Our last two billings were rife with errors—overbilling, double-billing, incorrect charges, that kind of thing. A lot of zeros popping up where they didn't belong."

"It might have been a software glitch." Jack sounded unconcerned. He crossed his arms.

Gracie tried to look interested in Hope's problems,

but Jack worried her more. Why had she suggested meeting at the Polska?

"Whatever it is—" Cliff's tone stiffened "—we've assured the insurance companies and clients that we'll fix the problem ASAP. I know LIT primarily creates medical information systems, but you've done updating and problem-solving before."

"Is that why you chose LIT?" Jack finally looked his dad in the eye.

Yes, Jack would want to know that. Gracie sipped her iced tea, praying God would pour oil over these troubled waters.

"Another Board member looked into possible companies to contact." Obviously not trusting the Polska's dishwasher, Cliff used a paper napkin to polish his tableware. "Anyway, he knew I had a son in information technology and called me to see if Lassater Information Tech was yours. He suggested we contact you."

Jack's lips thinned to a straight line. "So that's why you called?"

Gracie knew Cliff couldn't have said anything that would anger Jack more than this. According to Sandy, Jack hadn't even let Cliff pay for his son's college expenses.

"I didn't use my influence, if that's what you mean, Jack." Cliff's tone hardened. "Your reputation is excellent and the Board hoped that if you, with our family association, did the work, we could keep this under wraps. We don't want to lose credibility with our customers, make more out of this than we should. If customers begin to doubt a system, we could have people disputing charges. It would be a real mess.''

''I see.''

Gracie tried to read Jack's tone. Was he softening toward the idea of working for his dad or not?

''I'd like to have your answer today or by Friday at the latest. Our billing cycle waits for no man. And what if Medicare or Medicaid accounts are compromised this time? There could be fines, all kinds of legal fallout. And I don't even want to think about compromising of medical records. Who knows how far this will go if we don't stop it now?''

Jack frowned.

Gracie knew he didn't like to be pressured by clients. That was one of Tom's jobs—to keep the clients from irritating Jack. But this was an urgent situation and they needed the work.

''I think you've come to the right firm.'' Gracie spoke up in Tom's absence.

''We'll do it,'' Jack muttered.

Gracie swallowed an exclamation of surprise. Having Jack take the job had been what she'd wanted, but she'd expected to have to coax him. What had caused this turnaround?

At the front of the café, her sister Annie entered and glanced around.

Heads turned to look at her. News traveled fast in this neighborhood.

Gracie's pulse pounded in her temples.

Annie stalked toward her.

Gracie should be happy to see her sister, but Annie's stormy expression didn't reassure her.

Chapter Four

Later that evening in Sandy's driveway, Gracie opened the door of her dad's pickup and got out. Her mind whirred with vivid words and expressions from her intense confrontation with Annie in front of the Polska this afternoon.

"Come on, boys." Biting her lower lip, she motioned the twins to climb down from their seats at the rear of the extended cab.

"Is this where Mr. Lassater lives?" Austin asked, his eyes wide. He scrambled down onto the running board and then jumped with both feet to the sun-warmed asphalt.

His obvious excitement about seeing Jack again brought a lump to Gracie's throat. "You two, be on your best behavior," Gracie warned.

Why wouldn't Annie listen to me, Lord? How can she just step away from her sons?

Annie's accusation—''Why did you talk to Troy's mother about me?''—so unfair, still burned in Gracie's memory.

''We will!'' Andy promised, jumping down to join his brother.

Gracie's dad caught up with them at the front of the blue truck. ''Maybe we should have called first.'' He ran a hand around his waistband, tucking in his already tucked-in, freshly ironed shirt.

Gracie heard voices from the backyard. ''No, they're here. Sandy! Jack!'' she called from the driveway. ''It's me, Gracie…and company!''

With heavy heart, she led her ''men'' around the corner of the house to Sandy's small patio.

Jack and his mother sat on lawn chairs at a round table. The cooling evening breeze riffled the rain-stained fringe on the faded umbrella and the leaves on the nearby maple trees.

''Mike! Gracie! What a nice surprise!'' Sandy greeted the group as they came around the corner of her house. ''Mike, who do you have with you?''

Jack stood up. ''Mike?''

Gracie caught the confused expression Jack turned toward his mother, and paused for a moment. Hadn't Sandy told him? ''Jack, this is my dad, Mike Petrov. And you already know Austin and Andy.''

''Mr. Lassater! Hi!'' The twins dropped her hands

and charged Jack, wrapping their arms around his knees.

A palm on Austin's head, Jack shook hands with Mike and looked to Gracie, a question on his face. "I didn't expect to see you again today."

Gracie tried to smile, but his words only brought back the embarrassing scene. When Annie had shown up, Gracie had been forced to leave Jack alone with Cliff. She was sure they'd seen and overheard as much as everyone else at the Polska. Her sister had had no right to say what she did to Gracie. Annie had made it sound as if Gracie was siding with Troy against her. *I didn't cause this problem, Lord.*

And how had her unexpected departure affected the business deal with Hope?

"Please sit down," Sandy invited, motioning toward the remaining chairs.

Jack pulled out a chair for Gracie and then sat back down. Without hesitation, the boys clambered up on Jack, each settling on a knee. Jack ruffled their hair and grinned.

Handing Sandy a printed sheet, Mike dragged over a chair to sit right beside Sandy and her crutches. "I just wanted to bring over your building permit."

"Building permit?" Jack echoed, consternation in his tone.

"You got it already?" Beaming brightly like the molten-gold sun sinking below the treetops, Sandy accepted it. She acted as if she hadn't heard Jack.

"Yeah." Mike moved closer to Sandy, leaning

over her shoulder to view the document now in her hand. ''I'll post it on a tree in your front yard and I'll get started as soon as I wind up the final details on a couple of other jobs.''

Sandy gazed at the form, a broad smile on her face.

Ignoring a silent appeal from Jack, Gracie leaned over and tied Andy's loose shoelace. *Jack, I'm not explaining this. It's Sandy's job.*

''Mom—'' Jack started.

''Isn't this great, Jack?'' Sandy turned to her son. ''Mike gave me the best bid and even drew up the plans for me himself.''

''I… You never said anything…. I didn't know you'd gone this far with your plans.'' Jack looked displeased.

Gracie glanced at Sandy, who was turning pink.

''You're a busy man. And I can handle this.'' Sandy tapped Mike's arm, the one holding the building permit. ''Now, who are these two ragamuffins?''

Gracie kept her attention on her dad. He had an odd grin on his face. She'd thought it was funny that he wanted to drop over here tonight.

''They're my grandsons—'' Mike began.

''We're Austin and Andy!'' Austin announced. ''We came to see Mr. Lassater.''

Though Jack didn't look happy, he jiggled his knees, bouncing the boys and making them giggle.

''Mr. Lassater bought us candy bars,'' Andy confided.

"How nice." Sandy looked over to him. "Jack, that reminds me. Would you go in and get some refreshments for our guests?"

"No, Sandy—" Mike started to object.

"It's no problem, Mike," Sandy said, touching his arm again. "Jack will do it while I get acquainted with your grandsons. It's such a lovely evening and I've been cooped up here since Friday night with these crutches, though Jack has been keeping me company."

"Sure. I'll go get some iced tea," Jack said in a disgruntled voice that he didn't try to mask. He urged the twins down from his lap and stood up.

"Come here, boys." Mike held out his arms and the twins scrambled onto his lap.

Jack tried not to frown. The twins rushing to him had been as unexpected as it was satisfying. But how had this building permit happened without his knowing? And why did Gracie's dad have to sit so close to his mother? What was up with his mom?

Jack led Gracie into the kitchen. He stood at the counter pouring milk into plastic cups for the twins and then adding ice cubes to tall glasses and pouring tea. A fragrance that whispered "Gracie" was all around him.

"Are you wearing a new perfume or something?"

"No. In fact, I don't wear any perfume."

"Then, what do I smell?"

Gracie shook her head at him. "It's probably just my shampoo or soap."

"Oh." He wanted to say that it was a good scent. He liked it, but...

"You have the twins again."

Gracie folded her arms in front of her. "Annie's busy tonight working at her new job—she's a cashier at the student union cafeteria. And Troy went to talk to our minister. He doesn't know what to do."

She didn't sound happy. "How did your conversation with your sister go today?" he asked.

"It didn't go well." Gracie's face drooped into a deep frown.

"Why?" Jack's hand itched with the urge to touch her face. A weird sensation, another unexpected impulse.

"She was mad at me," Gracie explained, "because I've stayed home and taken care of the boys." She leaned her back against the counter. She looked a lot better than she had yesterday morning. Now, her hair fell in short dark waves around her face and she wore a fresh shorts outfit in fine red and white striped cotton.

He made himself consider what she'd just said. It didn't make sense. "I don't understand."

"My sister said that Troy should stay home and take care of them, not me."

He stared at her. "Is that why she left?"

Gracie lifted one shoulder. "No, but she said I don't know what's been going on between Troy and her—"

"Is she supporting herself with that job at the cafeteria?" Jack cut in.

"She got a grant and a scholarship and is living with two other women in a one-bedroom apartment near campus."

"And she wants her husband to quit work and stay home with their sons? Who's supposed to pay the rent and feed them?"

Gracie lifted both shoulders and then bowed her head. "Dad says I should keep my nose out of Annie's business. You know, no one knows what goes on behind closed doors. He says it's up to Troy and Annie to fix this. I just don't understand how she can justify moving out—leaving her children—over something like her going back to school."

Gracie's dark waves fell forward. He suppressed the unexpected urge to smooth them back so he could read her expression. "But…but you said Troy reneged on their deal. Maybe she didn't think she could do both."

Jack set the glasses on a tray. Golden rays from the setting sun pierced the mini-blinds over the sink and cast a halo on Gracie's hair and back. He paused, transfixed.

"She said that I didn't know what it was like being a wife and mother." Gracie continued the thread of their conversation as he stood, gazing at her. "She said Troy took her for granted—'devalued her,' as she put it—and she wasn't going to stand for it anymore. This just isn't like Annie. She's a great mom and I know she loves her kids more than anything else.''

''Well, she has funny ways of showing that.'' He opened the refrigerator and took out a lemon. *Why does Gracie look so different to me tonight?*

''Dad says that if Annie doesn't want me taking care of the boys, I have to let Troy put them in day care and come back to work.

''He did?''

''So I'll be back soon.'' She finally looked at him.

He handed the lemon to her since she stood between him and the sink. ''Wash this, please?''

As she reached for it, her arm brushed against his. A crazy buzz zipped up his arm.

Seemingly oblivious to her effect on him, she ran water over the yellow fruit and scrubbed it with her hands. ''Enough of my problems. Now I want to know why you said yes to your father's job.''

She'd switched topics on him, forcing him to face the decision he'd made. Jack frowned. ''It's hard to say.''

''Try.'' Gracie dropped the wet lemon into his palm.

He began slicing it into wedges. *Chink-chink,* the knife hit the cutting board. The lemon scent tickled his nose. *It's not just Gracie. Why am I so aware of everything tonight?* ''Just before I walked into the café this morning, I got a call from Tom in California.''

"That's right, you said he called. What did he want?" Gracie moved a step closer.

With the point of the knife, he flicked out the seeds of the lemon wedges. He concentrated on his explanation, not on Gracie so close to him. "Tom didn't say much, but he asked if I'd accepted my dad's job. When I asked him why, all he'd say was that nothing ever stays the same and that I should take the job."

"Nothing ever stays the same?" Gracie repeated, tucking in her chin. She stared downward.

"Tom's phone call gave me…a funny feeling." Jack glanced at Gracie's slender, shapely legs and swallowed the sudden thickness in his throat. "I can't put my finger on it, but I just felt I should take the Hope Medical job."

"That's interesting." She turned to face him. Taking another step closer, she lowered her voice. "But I know what you mean. I had an odd feeling last Friday night when Tom stopped in right before his flight. There was something he was holding back from us."

He nodded and lifted a small glass bowl from the cabinet above. Only inches separated them. He inhaled the citrus and her scent, a delicious combination.

Taking the bowl, Gracie began arranging the lemon wedges in it. "When will Hope sign our contract?"

Jack looked out the window to keep from watching her deft hands. "I faxed their central office our standard contract and Dad said he'd have the Hope lawyer go over it and get back to me if they want any changes.''

"Okay, then. We have a new project, I'll be back to work no later than Monday, and we both have a funny feeling about Tom." Gracie placed the bowl of lemon wedges on the tray.

"How did my mom connect with your dad?" He picked up the tray.

"One day when she stopped by on her lunch break from the library, she mentioned that she needed an addition to her house and some changes, such as enlarging doorways in case she needs a walker or wheelchair in the future.''

Jack felt his insides congeal at the thought of what his mother might face in the future. "I'm staying here until she's off crutches. I guess I should be glad of the Hope job, since your dad already has gotten Mom's building permit. I'd hoped I'd have more time to get together the capital to pay for the changes she needs. Or better yet, I wanted to try one more time to get her to sell this and move into a ranch-style—''

Gracie shook her head. "I think your mom's right to stay in her neighborhood. If she needs help—''

"I'm the one who should help her.''

"Of course. But I think your mom wants to help herself, keep her independence and her pride…in being able to handle this herself. Early retirement has to be hard to swallow for a woman so young.'' Gracie rested her hand on his sleeve.

An electric-like current raced up his arm from her touch. He glanced down.

Gracie removed her hand as if self-conscious. ''I'm glad you took the Hope job. It sounds like your dad needs your help, too.''

The shocking sensation of her touch lingered in his arm. He focused on it, rather than on the irritation he felt at being obligated to help his dad in order to get money to help his mom.

Before Jack could reply, his cell phone rang. Handing Gracie the tray, he slipped the phone off his belt and answered.

''Jack?'' his father said.

''Yes.''

His father's voice came clipped as though he were in a hurry. ''I want you to come to a Hope Board member's house tomorrow evening. It's a pool party. Dress casual.''

''Pool party!'' he exclaimed. *I don't do business at pool parties.*

''Yes, the Board members want to meet you socially before we sign the contract.''

''Why can't I just come to your offices or you come to mine?'' Jack stalled.

''A few members want to ask you just how undercover you can do the job for us. They're concerned about security.''

Somebody's paranoid. "This isn't necessary—" Jack started.

"Someone may be sabotaging our system. We've been careful not to send any of our plans to solve it via e-mail. We need this to be discreet." His dad rattled off the address and hung up.

Fuming, Jack snapped his phone shut and turned to Gracie. "Do you own a bathing suit?"

The sound of splashing water and laughter made Gracie lean close to Jack's ear so he would hear her. "Be polite," she reminded him. "Smile. Answer questions with non-geeky words. Ask if anyone has any questions, okay?"

He exhaled laboriously. "Okay."

Gracie knew that anyone who overheard her would think she was bonkers, but Jack—the penultimate, non-user-friendly computer guru—needed these reminders. *Especially with Tom, our Mr. Charm, away in San Francisco.*

Jack knew Gracie meant well and he appreciated her giving him pointers. He was used to having Tom with him to interpret his technical explanations to "non-computer" people. But he wanted to know— was this all a big mistake? Was this meeting about computer problems at a pool party—of all places— just another ploy by his dad to involve him not only in his business but in his life?

But most of all, why had Gracie worn a bright yellow swimsuit tonight? Her legs moving under the short skirt of green with yellow swirls distracted him, made him edgy.

Their hostess, Mrs. Dunn, a too-thin surgeon's wife, informed them her husband was a *head* surgeon and led them to the other guests. At one end of the oval pool, a group of well-tanned doctors and their spouses lounged on patio furniture.

Jack's dad stood up. "This is my son, Jack, and his executive assistant, Gracie." Cliff went around the group of doctors, introducing everyone, all in crisp shorts or swimsuits and tropical wraps.

Jack shook hands and forced a smile. Then he and Gracie sat down facing the Hope group, their backs to the pool. "Okay, what do you want to know?"

Cliff chuckled. "I told you my son's all business."

Gracie rested her arm on the deck chair's armrest and dangled her slim wrist over its edge.

Jack again wondered why he kept noticing things about Gracie. *We've worked together for years. Is it this meeting that's put me on edge?*

A female doctor sat forward in her chair. "I'm Dr. Sarah Brown. I'd like to get an idea of what you think you can do to solve our problems."

At Gracie's cue, a clearing of her throat, Jack nodded, acknowledging the woman's question. "It's hard to say." He remembered to smile. "I haven't had a chance to look over your software and the damage already done to your system."

"Do you think it's the work of a hacker?" another doctor asked.

"I can't say." Jack shrugged. "But do you have any idea why someone would want to tamper with your system?"

"A few people have asked me the same question," said a distinguished-looking doctor with silver hair and broad shoulders, not looking at anyone but Jack.

At the man's words, Jack felt a coldness that overwhelmed the people around him. "I'm sorry. I'm not good with names." He lifted his eyebrows in question.

"I'm Dr. Harry Collins. And everyone on the Board will tell you that my consuming hobby is computers. I tried to get the Board to hire someone like you over two years ago. But no one would listen to me."

Again, an uncomfortable silence—one so pointed that Jack couldn't mistake it.

"Hindsight is always twenty-twenty," Grace murmured.

The tension eased and Jack relaxed in his chair. "Another thing—what my dad has described is the type of damage research labs or financial institutions might experience. Has anyone asked themselves why Hope has been targeted? What information do you have that someone might want and for what purpose? Or who might have the intent to harm your reputation?"

No one spoke. They just stared at him.

Suddenly, *splash!* Water cascaded over the assembly at the end of the pool. The women nearest the pool squealed and covered their hair and faces.

Gracie chuckled and ran her hands through her hair, which curled up with the moisture. Gracie's trim arms suddenly fascinated Jack.

Their hostess, Mrs. Dunn, stood up and strode to the poolside. "Boys! I told you, no cannonballs while the adults are meeting!"

"Sorry." About five kids around junior high age climbed out. "We didn't know we were this close to the diving board," an especially thin kid added. Then they all dived, one by one, back into the deep end but without much splashing.

Gracie fluffed up her damp hair and then let her arms drift back to where they'd been. A bead of water dripped from her hair, trailing down her soft cheek.

Tensing, Jack stopped himself from brushing away the droplet.

"Back to business," Cliff said, "I don't think any of us have come up with a motive for this. Has anyone?" He glanced around.

"No." Dr. Dunn spoke up, facing Jack.

"No disgruntled computer-savvy employees?" Jack probed, feeling that they were holding something back from him. "No one with a grudge against Hope? Any business rivals who would benefit if your system is discredited and audited?"

"No," Dr. Brown said.

Jack felt Gracie's attention on him. An unusual

warmth rose through him. "Anyone who has sued Hope and not gotten what they thought they deserved?"

Frowns on most faces appeared in the lowering light of evening. Dr. Collins, Jack noted, sat with his arms folded as if separated from the group and this discussion.

"Maybe," Cliff conceded.

"It might pay you to give me the names of anyone you suspect of having a grudge against Hope. I can always do a covert computer check on them and see if they are up to something."

"You can do that?" A young voice came from behind Jack.

Jack craned his neck around. The other kids climbed out dripping and giggling and joined the kid who'd asked the question. "Yeah, I can."

"Cool." The kid, along with the others, dived back into the pool.

The doctors and their wives chuckled, lightening the atmosphere.

"That was our son," Mrs. Dunn said. "It's a new generation. Damon had to explain to me last week what an MP3 player was."

Jack wondered if the kids would have a better grasp of the problem than the secretive group of doctors and spouses he was addressing. *They're not telling me something.*

"You should all take more interest in what's happening in software," Dr. Collins said in an odd, challenging voice. "You'll all be left behind...as I told you more than once."

"I can't keep up with everything!" Dunn snapped. "I have enough just keeping up with what's happening in my field and taking care of patients. You don't have a family, Harry. Everything takes time. And we can take care of this computer problem just as we have—by hiring an expert."

Murmurs of agreement followed this. Dr. Collins rose and stalked away.

Lights around the pool came on automatically, probably due to a light sensor or timer.

Gracie smiled. "Any more questions?"

Jack looked from face to face. No one replied. "Then, I will give you one more warning." He pressed his lips together. "No system is impregnable. I will go through your software and see what has caused this problem. Then I'll go through your archived files to see where and how the hacker—if there is one—has gotten into the system and devise new ways to keep him or her out."

One said, "A female hacker! We hadn't thought of that!"

Another commented, "Equal rights in hacking."

Jack ignored them. This wasn't a humorous matter. "Remember, I'll need a list of possible suspects."

"No problem." Cliff rose. "I'll make sure you get it."

"Then, after my preliminary examination, I'll

most likely design a new software accounting program for you and then assign all new passwords. If you have a glitch or someone decides to hack into your files for the fun of it, those measures should be enough. I could design you a high-security system, something that a defense lab would require, but I don't think you need anything that elaborate.'' Jack lifted his hand. ''That's it.''

The group gazed at him.

Gracie cleared her throat.

Jack smiled on cue as he became aware that Gracie now stood at his elbow. He glanced at her. She gave him a dazzling smile and he warmed at her approval.

''Great!'' Cliff said. ''Sounds like you have what we need. We'll get together with our lawyers and finalize the contract.''

Most of the men surged out of their seats and shook Jack's hand. A few slapped him on the back. He smiled politely, realizing just how tense he had been over this and how relaxed Gracie appeared. After congratulating themselves on hiring him, they moved away toward a bar and table of refreshments.

''Want to swim now?'' Gracie asked at his elbow. Then she leaned toward his ear. ''Good job,'' she murmured. ''Tom couldn't have done better.''

Before Jack could reply, his cell phone rang. He lifted it from the pocket of his shorts. ''Hello.''

''Hi, Jack, it's Tom. I'm on my way home from O'Hare.''

"Tom? You're back early." Jack watched Gracie shrug out of the wrap skirt over her bathing suit.

"Right. I've got news. It couldn't wait. See you first thing tomorrow." Tom hung up.

Gazing at Gracie's trim waist, Jack said with difficulty, "It was Tom. He'll be in the office tomorrow morning."

Gracie slipped off her sandals. "Well, at least we'll find out if there is something funny or if he just landed us another job."

Jack shoved his phone into his shirt pocket and then took off the shirt and draped it over his chair back. "Which will be really irritating now that we've taken on this project."

Gracie laughed at him and dove into the pool.

He couldn't take his eyes off her as she swam away, her slender form and white skin outlined by the underwater pool lights.

Chapter Five

$\sim$

The next morning, Gracie perched at her computer station at the LIT office and stared at the file name "Sassafras." A mere six days ago, she'd started her letter of resignation. But those six days had been so full of changes and frayed tempers that the short passage of time felt painfully prolonged.

She tapped a key and opened the file. She scanned her beginning and then placed her hands over the keys, ready to finish the letter. She paused and glanced at the newspaper beside her computer.

She'd set the classified job section of the *Chicago Tribune* there. Earlier, she'd scanned the offerings for executive assistants. Not one had piqued her interest. The exercise had only depressed her.

Just because Annie had moved out and Jack had taken a job for his father's corporation didn't change anything about her needing to resign. She closed her eyes and wished she could convince herself of that. Deep down, however, her spirit rebelled against adding one more ounce of stress to this disastrous mix.

"Hey!" Tom sang out. He threw open the office door with a very Tom flourish. A few steps and he parked himself on the front corner of her desk. "Gracie, my sweetheart, how've you been?" Then he bent over, caught her face in his hands and kissed her.

"Tom!" she protested, flushing warmly.

"Cut it out," Jack growled from the doorway behind Tom. "We can't afford to lose Gracie over a charge of sexual harassment."

Tom chuckled. "If you had any sense, Jack, you'd propose to this amazing woman. If you don't, you're going to lose her someday—and what would you do without her?"

Gracie froze inside. Had Tom guessed how she felt about Jack? Had she betrayed her love without realizing it?

"I like Gracie too much to spoil our working relationship with marriage," Jack said in a grumpy voice. He entered the room, his hands shoved into his pockets. "So what's up, Tom?"

Jack's careless comment stung, but Gracie made no reply. She prickled with the charged currents eddying around her. Gazing up at Tom, she tracked Jack's movement and dour expression from the corner of her eye. Jack had dressed all in black. Funereal.

Tom glanced at Jack and then to her. He smiled broadly. "I hope you both will be happy for me."

"Why?" Jack lowered himself onto one of their new leather couches. "Did *you* propose to someone?"

Uncertainty fluttered in Gracie's midsection.

Tom chuckled. "In a way. I've finally figured out what makes me happy and how to make sure I stay that way."

Jack lifted one eyebrow.

"Speak English," Gracie said, aggravation now humming along her nerve endings.

Tom laughed. "Okay, I finally realized why I've been so restless over the past year."

"Restless?" Jack stared at Tom. "I don't know what you're talking about."

"I've noticed it," she murmured.

Jack looked tense, ready to spring.

Gracie fidgeted with the papers on her desk.

Tom grinned.

Jack looked to her and then back at Tom. *"So?"*

"So, I finally realized what I enjoy—" Tom motioned broadly, extravagantly "—is the challenge of *launching* a new business. That's what got me excited at the end of our college days together. You had a vision of your own information tech company. *I* had a vision of performing a modern miracle in helping 'Mr. Computer Whiz But Don't Bother Me with Customers' get it launched and profitable. That was what made my blood pump!"

"What's your point?" Jack leveled both his eyes and this question at Tom, his tone unimpressed.

"You succeeded. I succeeded. LIT has an enviable reputation." Tom shrugged. "And you don't need me anymore."

Cold dread rolled through Gracie like a snowball tumbling downhill, gathering size with each turn. *No, Tom, don't leave!*

"The heck I don't," Jack snapped. "You know how I feel about meeting with customers. I can't be bothered. It burns up my working time. I had to take Gracie with me twice this week to do *your* job. Besides, you're my partner. LIT is yours, too. Doesn't that mean anything to you?"

Gracie inhaled deeply. Yes, Jack would take Tom leaving as personal.

"Don't get hot under the collar," Tom taunted, but with a smile. "Of course LIT means something to me. It was my first success! But I can't stay here any longer, just doing the same old schmoozing. It doesn't satisfy me. You just said that Gracie already took over part of my job—running interference between you and our customers. Gracie can do that."

"No!" Tom's suggestion forced the word out of her. She couldn't do what Tom did. "I'm just the executive assistant." *And I'm leaving as soon as things get back to normal.*

"Ha!" Tom said in a sardonic tone. "Don't underestimate yourself, Gracie. You're much more than that. You're the person who keeps LIT afloat and organized.''

"Darn right she is,'' Jack agreed while still glaring at Tom.

The praise, especially Jack's, caught her off guard. She felt her face blaze with embarrassment.

"Any intelligent person could do what I've been doing for LIT over the last couple of years,'' Tom continued. "Don't you see? I need a new project, a new business to promote. That's what excites me.''

Silence.

Gracie and Jack stared at Tom and then Gracie glanced to Jack and found him looking back at her. She read the plea in his troubled blue eyes.

"Tom,'' she implored, "tell us what you are planning to do.''

"I've signed on to promote a new techno genius in the game sector of the market—'' Tom started.

"Games!'' Jack spat out.

"Yes, I know you think that's beneath me. But the company and the games they're coming up with—''

"But you're my partner!'' Jack interrupted Tom, nearly jumping up from his seat. "If you leave, I'll have to buy you out. It could end up destroying LIT—''

"Hold it!'' Tom held up both his hands. "I've already figured that problem out. Hear what I have to say.''

Jack looked to Gracie again. A vein in his neck pulsed.

She nodded at him, pursing her lips.

"Okay, spit it out." Jack folded his arms over his chest and glowered at Tom.

"I've already convinced my new company that they should move their base of operations to Chicago. The overhead here is so much lower. So I was thinking that instead of buying me out with cash, you could let me have this office, the lease and everything that goes with it. And, of course, you would add some shares to my LIT stock. That way you wouldn't have to buy me with cash."

Jack frowned. "Where would we work, then?"

Tom lifted both hands. "That's up to you and Gracie." He nodded toward her. "LIT's established. You don't need an imposing address. My new fledgling company does."

Tom rose from her desk. "So that's my big news. I've got a lot to do today, so I'll leave and let you two mull it over. Get back to me soon." Tom waved to them and was out the door.

Gracie realized her mouth was open and closed it. Another blow. Annie leaving, now Tom. *I should be leaving, too.*

She glanced at her screen and tapped a few keys, deleting her "Sassafras" file. Then she leaned her head into her hand. Jack was a genius with computers, but not with people! He needed her now.

Later that afternoon, back in his own office again, Jack stared at the ever-changing red, blue and gold patterns flickering on his monitor. After Tom's visit, Jack had spent the day at Hope's central financial office, going over computer files, piecing together whatever evidence he could. What he'd found hadn't been reassuring.

Some Board members had stopped by during the day and submitted a few names of possible suspects. One name had popped up in every discussion so far—all with requests for discretion. Dr. Collins, whom he'd met at the pool party, had been ousted as Board chair in the spring. Everyone reminded Jack that Collins's hobby was computers. But, of course, it couldn't be Harry.

Jack hadn't thought this much of a lead until he checked out Collins's own PC security. Impressive. And slightly suspicious. What was Dr. Collins afraid someone might find on his system?

Dark thoughts and suspicion swirled in Jack's mind before giving way to his main concern. "What am I going to do about Tom?" he muttered. He stood up, stretched his tight muscles. He walked over and looked out his office window. Down below, old Louis was selling a businessman a newspaper. *Today's Thursday.*

Just last Friday night, he'd stopped to chat with the old guy about the Cubs—not a worry in the world. How could he have known the earth was going to shift on its axis? What *hadn't* happened since that night?

His mother had fallen and injured herself. Gracie

was having personal problems. His dad had forced his way back into Jack's life with the Hope contract. Jack paused, turning back toward his monitor. *Too late to back out. Mom needs the money the Hope job will bring in.*

Gracie stepped into his office. "Jack, I'm leaving now—unless you need me for anything."

He gazed at her. She wore one of her sober gray suits. A white collar buttoned tight at her neck. He envisioned her as she'd looked last night. Her pale shoulders and slender form as she dived into the pool… He hauled his thoughts back to the present.

Besides, Gracie faced her own crisis with her sister deserting her family. He thought of Austin and Andy, one with a mole and one without. "Who's been taking care of the twins today?" He couldn't keep the sharpness out of his tone.

"Troy enrolled them in a day care near our neighborhood. Our pastor knew of an opening." Gracie didn't sound or look happy. "While I was gone this week, things piled up. I've spent all day getting my projects back in order. How did it go at Hope?"

He shook his head. "Not good. It's not a glitch in the software or incompetent staff. Someone's been fiddling with their data."

Her shoulders slumped and she sighed. "A hacker?"

Her sympathy was welcome. He nodded glumly. "If they'd called me right in, I might have found enough evidence to get some idea of who penetrated the system and how. But their people had gone through opening files—and you know that overwrites whatever footprints the hacker left behind.''

''Did you tell them to freeze the systems if anything else occurs?'' Gracie leaned against the doorjamb.

It was an unusual pose for her. An unprecedented physical reaction to her rippled through him. He tried to ignore it. ''I *personally* told everyone in the office 'hands off,' and sent out a red-alert memo to everyone who accesses the files. We'll see if they have enough sense to do what I say.'' Jack doubted it.

She put out a hand as though beckoning him. ''Wouldn't someone have to know their encryption in order to—''

Jack snorted with disdain. ''Their computer security system was done five years ago—a century in computer time.'' He stepped around his desk. ''It was laughable, except no one's laughing now. Least of all me.''

Gracie nodded and lowered her head. ''Have you done any thinking about Tom's proposal?''

He shoved his hands through his hair. ''I haven't had a minute. What do you think we should do?''

She folded her arms. ''Do we have a choice? Tom's not just your business partner. He's a friend. If he wants to leave, how could we—you—try to stop him?''

Jack had no answer. He leaned his hip against the

corner of his cluttered desk. The truth of what she said was too obvious.

"Well, I'll see you tomorrow." Gracie pushed off from the doorjamb. "Before you get started at Hope on Friday, will you check in with me here either by phone or in person? And I've left a few items on my desk that need your signature." She turned halfway, ready to depart.

He nodded and let her go. Reversing direction, he bypassed his desk and computer. Back at the window, he stared down, waiting for...

Below, Gracie sauntered outside. She shrugged out of her jacket and tossed it over her shoulder. She hooked it there with her upraised hand. It was a jaunty, free gesture. The sight released a strange tension he'd been scarcely aware of. He couldn't tear himself away from the window as she headed toward the bus stop. He watched until Gracie vanished from view.

His mind conjured up how she'd looked in her father's kitchen, at the Polska Café, in his mother's backyard and at the pool party in that bathing suit.

He'd never seen Gracie wearing casual clothes before this week. In the office, she always wore dark suits with white blouses, very much the sober businesswoman. How could he have guessed how... intriguing she'd be in different clothing and in atypical settings.

A thought popped into his head. He pondered it. Would this idea work with Gracie?

* * *

As Gracie walked through the front gate of home, she heard cheerful voices in the backyard. The moist heat of the day weighed on her. Her pantyhose suffocated her—torture! All she wanted to do was get into shorts.

She hurried up the steps and inside. Someone waited for her in the doorway in the foyer.

"Patience!" Gracie shrieked and ran forward to embrace her cousin. "We didn't expect you until Saturday."

Patience hugged her back. "I managed to get things wrapped up early at my apartment, and here I am home, ready to hunt for a job."

Within minutes they were in her bedroom, Gracie peeling off her business uniform while Patience perched on Gracie's bed, answering questions about job prospects. Then they strolled out to the backyard, drawn by the aroma of a charcoal fire in the grill.

Mike greeted them as he opened the grill lid. "So you made it home on time for a change."

Before Gracie could reply, she noticed someone else she hadn't expected to see. "Sandy! I didn't— How are you?"

Pink tinged Sandy's cheeks. "Mike insisted I join you for this celebration of your cousin's homecoming."

"I'm glad he did. Are you walking better?" Gracie eased onto a lawn chair, buried her bare feet in the sun-warmed grass and tried to figure out why

Sandy was blushing. Maybe she thought they might assume that she was pursuing Mike. But that wasn't likely. Her dad hadn't dated since Mom died. He probably felt bad that Sandy was housebound.

"I'm fine—" Sandy started.

"I dropped off some building materials in her garage." Mike closed the grill lid with a dull *clang*. "And since who knows when her son will decide to come home, I thought she might as well celebrate with us." With a grin, he lifted a tall glass of lemonade and toasted Patience.

Patience lifted her own glass in response. Her cousin was Gracie's exact opposite—tall, blond and intellectual. And now a straight-A graduate with a degree in education.

"I'm glad you came, Sandy." Gracie took a sip of her own lemonade. "And I'm sure you'll be glad when you can get about easier."

"My ankle is already less swollen and feels better. I think I'll be off my crutches next week—"

"You be careful," Mike cautioned. "Don't push yourself too hard."

"Sandy, have you talked to Jack today?" Gracie asked.

"No, but I didn't expect to." Sandy cocked her head to one side as though questioning Gracie.

So he didn't call and tell you about Tom. Hmm. Gracie pondered this.

"I'm so glad you talked him into taking the job for his dad," Sandy continued.

Gracie worried her lower lip. *Should I mention Tom—?*

"Hey!" Jack's voice carried from the side of the house. "Don't you people answer your doorbell?"

Gracie sat up straighter. Jack? Here again?

"Come on back!" her dad called.

Jack sauntered around the corner of the house. He hadn't changed from the office. His black slacks and shirt stood out as alien amid the greens, pinks and gold of the summer backyard.

He stopped. "*Mom?* What are you doing here?"

Gracie heard his displeasure and watched him stiffen.

Sandy blushed a brighter pink. "I left you a note telling you where I was. Didn't you see it on the kitchen table?"

"I haven't been home." Jack stared at his mother, his thumbs hooked into his pockets.

Gracie stood up. "Jack, I don't think you've met my cousin, Patience Andrews. We're celebrating her homecoming after college."

Jack stared at his mother. He didn't flicker an eyelash.

Recognizing his signs of preoccupation, Gracie cleared her throat, giving him his cue. *Come on, Jack.*

With a smile, he came forward and offered Patience his hand. "Nice to meet you, Patience."

Dear Lord, how can I leave him to manage customers alone? What is this man going to do without

Tom? Without me? He can't do it alone. I can't leave
LIT now.

"I've always wanted to meet you," Patience said.
"Your job must be fascinating. What are you working on now?"

"I can't really give details." Jack walked toward
Gracie, but was still focused on his mother who was
sitting beside Mike. "It's a security problem."

Gracie closed the distance between them, wanting
to shake him. This unnecessary possessiveness toward his mother wasn't attractive at all.

"Oh dear," Sandy said. "Is it very difficult?"

Jack nodded, still staring from his mother to Gracie's dad. "I'll be putting in a lot of days and nights
on it. It's an interesting puzzle."

Gracie touched Jack's arm, trying to tell him to sit
down, but he didn't appear to even notice. She let
her hand drop.

"Well—" her dad spoke up "—we're pleased
you joined us and I'm relieved I bought a few extra
steaks. Gracie, get Jack something to drink."

"Okay, Dad." Gracie turned and walked up the
back porch steps. She felt Jack following her and was
glad. She didn't want him upsetting his mother over
nothing.

As soon as the back door shut behind them, Gracie
whirled.

Jack bumped into her.

Her pulse raced, making her feel out of breath.
"What brought you here tonight?" she asked with

an effort to hide her physical response to him. "Did Tom call back or has something happened with Hope?"

"No." Jack brushed her questions away with a wave of his hand. Without warning, he claimed her shoulders with both hands.

She held her breath, thoughts ricocheting through her mind.

"I wanted to ask you a question," he said.

With his full attention on her, she waited. Finally, when he didn't speak, she prompted, "What question?"

Jack looked away. "Would you take over Tom's job?"

She gaped at him, open-mouthed.

"Well?" he coaxed, gripping her shoulders more firmly. "Would you?"

She jerked out of his hold and swept into the kitchen. She flung open the refrigerator door. "Is that supposed to be a joke?"

"No." He trailed right behind her. "I've thought over what Tom said earlier. He said you could do part of his job—"

"Just running interference for you with customers." Gracie felt more than the stifling heat from the day. She burned with irritation. "I don't have a business degree in marketing and sales like Tom does." She sloshed Jack a glass of lemonade and shoved it into his hand.

"Well, LIT has an established reputation now.

Tom said that we didn't need an office on Michigan Avenue anymore to impress customers. And I don't need a marketing genius like Tom anymore. He was right. Word of mouth brings us most customers now. That's why he must want to leave LIT. I get it now. Remember, Hope came to us.''

"But there was a family connection,'' she snapped. "They knew that you were Cliff's son.''

"That wasn't why they hired me!'' Jack raised his voice, too. "You're good with people.'' He tossed this compliment at her even in the midst of arguing with her. "You know the business as well as Tom does. You're perfect for the position.''

Gracie's heart thudded with dread. "I'm just your executive assistant. I can't do Tom's job.'' She turned her back to him and folded her arms. *Unfair, Jack!*

"Well, you're going to,'' he said. "I don't have time to look for another partner.'' His tone became gritty. "This Hope project is going to consume me until I get the system cleaned up and secure again.''

"Jack—''

"Gracie, there's no time.'' He swung her around to face him.

"I'm not—''

"I'm not taking no for an answer.'' Jack pulled her toward him.

"Then, I quit.'' She pushed him away.

Mike opened the door and stepped into the kitchen. "What's going on here?'' he demanded.

Jack's expression was stormy, almost belligerent. "I want Gracie to move up in LIT and take on more responsibility—"

"I can't," Gracie persisted. "Don't ask me—!"

"Let Jack talk, Gracie. What are you offering her?"

Gracie clenched her fists at her sides. Jack's nearness heightened her negative reaction to this preposterous suggestion.

Jack turned to Mike. "I want her to meet with customers, negotiate deals and help with customer relations."

"Dad, Tom has quit—" Gracie started.

"That sounds like a job you'd be good at, Gracie," her dad said. "Why don't you want to take it?"

She brushed past Jack. His bare arm grazed her. Her pulse spiked. "Dad," she said, appealing directly to him, "it takes a business degree in marketing and sales to do the job—"

"No, it doesn't," Jack said, his tone becoming urgent, "You think that's why I took Tom on as a partner?"

"Wasn't it?" Gracie looked up into his intense eyes.

"No, Tom and I went to high school and college together. We were friends, good ones."

Jack's tone implored her. "When we were seniors, I told him what I wanted to do and he said, 'Let's go for it.' He found us a few backers and then went out and drummed up our first client.''

"I can't...I couldn't..." Gracie stammered.

"I don't need you to do that starting-up stuff now,'' Jack said. "LIT is a known business. You just need to represent LIT with people who seek us out. I can hire a publicist if I need one. Gracie, no one knows our business better than you. I need you. And you can do it.''

"He's right,'' Mike said, and left them, closing the door behind him.

After dark, Jack drove his mother to her house.

"That was quite an evening,'' his mom commented, then sighed. "I've never seen Gracie so worked up. She could barely sit still.''

"Yeah.'' But Gracie's negative reaction didn't claim Jack's attention. He wanted to ask, *So what's with you turning up at Gracie's house?* But he couldn't. He didn't know what his mom would answer and he was afraid she'd say something he didn't want to hear. His stomach clenched.

"Mike's almost ready to start on my addition.'' Sandy released her seat belt, seeming oblivious to Jack's agitation.

"Let me know the amount of the deposit he needs to get started,'' Jack managed to say as he opened his door. He'd meant to discuss this with her, but he'd been inundated with other concerns.

"Oh, I won't need any help from you, dear. I've

been saving up for this for a long time and I've already applied for a home equity loan to make up the difference.''

Jack froze. *Then why did I take the Hope job?*

Chapter Six

The next morning at Annie's college, Gracie eased inside the cool brick and marble building. Like a spy in a foreign land. Laughing, giggling and chatting, college kids in shorts, sandals, halter tops and T-shirts streamed around her, entering and leaving the student union building.

Inside the entrance she halted, feeling extremely out of place in her dark business suit. She scouted the area and found a directory. Then she headed downstairs to the cafeteria in the basement. According to their dad, Annie should be finishing up her part-time shift there about now.

Gracie waited in the cafeteria entrance, scanning the sparsely populated tables for her sister. The twin scents of bacon and cinnamon rolls filled the air.

Then Gracie's eyes widened. Annie sauntered toward her. But her sister was not alone. Her face turned away from Gracie, she strolled beside a handsome young man. She was looking up at him and laughing. As though she didn't have two little boys at home crying for their mother.

"Annie." The name sounded and felt wrenched from Gracie.

Annie halted, antagonism replacing shock in her expression.

Plainly ill at ease, the young man hovered. He cleared his throat. "Anything wrong, Ann Marie?"

Annie smiled at him. "No, go on. I'll see you in class."

The young man loped off.

Annie closed the gap between them, stopping right in front of Gracie. "What are you doing here?"

To say the question sounded hostile was an understatement. Gracie stalled. What could she say to ease past her sister's obvious annoyance?

"I miss you." The words slipped off her tongue before she thought them through, but they were the right words. Gracie recalled one of her mother's favorite verses: "A soft word turneth away wrath."

Annie's face softened. "I miss you, too, Gracie."

The two sisters who'd lived under the same roof all their lives stared at one another, uncomfortable and uncertain. Gracie saw this in Annie's eyes and felt it inside herself.

"How are you?" *I can't believe I'm saying this to Annie.*

"I'm fine, Sis. How are you?"

Reeling with the unreality of this moment, Gracie shrugged. How was she? "Jack's gone crazy. He wants me to take over Tom's position at LIT."

That's not what I meant to say. The words seemed to have bubbled up without warning. She had come to talk some sense into her sister, not to talk about her own problems.

"Wow, that is some news." Annie studied Grace. "Come on. Walk me to class."

Gracie fell into step beside her sister.

"What happened to Tom?" Annie had changed her hair, which used to fall loose to her shoulders, into two spiky pigtails.

Gracie wondered where Annie had come up with her new outfit. She never wore hip-hugger shorts and flaunted a bare midriff. "Tom's taking on the launch of another hi-tech company. And he's leaving LIT."

"When did that happen?" In her Birkenstock sandals, Annie set a brisk pace.

"Yesterday." Too brisk a pace for Gracie. She wished she weren't wearing a new pair of business heels.

"This is so cool, Sis. It's about time you crawled out of your shell." Annie grinned at her. "You'll do great—"

"Annie, you know I'm not qualified for the position—" Gracie said with as much force as she could muster. *I'm not brilliant like you and Jack.*

"Why not take it?" Annie lifted her newly

plucked eyebrows. "Jack must think you're qualified."

Annie was wearing eye makeup. Troy hated makeup.

"I don't have the education I'd need to be Jack's representative. I only have a piddly two-year associate degree."

"So what? You've been with LIT from day one. You know more than you think you do!"

Annie's praise and confidence in Gracie were unexpected and persuasive, but... "I couldn't do it. Jack asked me because he just doesn't want to take the time and energy to locate a replacement for Tom."

"Stop." Annie frowned and shook her head at Gracie. "If you start trying to find someone to replace you, I'll bean you! You've got to start believing in yourself and just do it. I know. I speak from experience."

"What experience?" Gracie asked in a cautious tone. *Annie, tell me why you left.*

Annie shut down before her eyes. "You don't need to know," she said through tight lips. "That's between me and Troy."

"What's going on? You never said anything to me or Dad to warn us. Why did you have to leave?"

Annie sped up. "Don't mother me, Gracie. I'm twenty-three now and an adult."

Gracie kept up with her. The shoes chafed her heels the way Annie's attitude chafed her heart. Of course Gracie had tried to mother Annie, who'd only been ten when their mother died. *I did my best for you, Annie.*

"This is between me and Troy," Annie repeated.

"But what about the twins? It concerns them." Gracie heard the pleading in her tone.

"Tell that to Troy," Annie said, eyes blazing. "He tried to guilt me into dropping my classes and coming home. But it won't work. He didn't send you, did he?"

"No one had to send me. I'm concerned. About the twins and Troy and you. Why did you have to leave? Why couldn't you just go to school this fall like you'd planned?" *Why is all this happening! Can't anything go right this summer?*

"Because I couldn't take it anymore!" Annie rounded on her. "Troy and I had a deal and he reneged. In fact, he reneged twice."

"Twice?"

"Yes, you know—" Annie held the books in her arms like a shield "—he promised before we married that I'd go to college the fall after my high school graduation—"

"But he didn't know you'd get...you'd be expecting the boys so soon," Gracie pointed out.

"The heck he didn't."

"Annie, you're not serious?"

"Yes, I am. I heard, overheard...something...." Annie fell silent. She started walking again, nearly marching.

Gracie clicked along, her heels raw. The hot sunshine caused a trickle of perspiration down the side of her face.

With a clenched jaw, Annie continued in a dark tone. "And ever since I knew I was pregnant, Troy has done everything he could to keep me home, and for what? I've sacrificed and sacrificed for the boys, while Troy thinks just bringing home a paycheck is all he has to do as their father." Annie paused in front of an imposing limestone building. "My class is in here. I'm late." She turned and raced up the steps.

"Annie," Gracie called after her, "your sons need you. Won't you come for supper tonight and see them?"

"Can't." Annie turned back and glared at her. "Troy says I shouldn't visit until I'm ready to come home for good and be his obedient house-frau again. He says my visit would just upset Austin and Andy—" Annie's voice broke with tears.

"He said that?" Gracie asked.

But Annie disappeared inside the heavy metal and glass double doors.

Gracie slowly walked toward an empty park bench a few feet away. She sank down onto it. Annie's words whirled, revolved, spun in her mind—

"Are you okay, lady?"

Gracie looked up.

A student, arms filled with books, glanced down

at her. His brow furrowed. "You look like you're not feeling too good."

"Thanks." Gracie sat up straighter. "I'm fine. I just got some bad news and it shook me up a little."

He nodded, still eyeing her. "Would you like me to walk you to the visitor parking, ma'am?"

Ma'am? I look like a ma'am? Must be the suit. "Thanks, no. I came on the bus."

"Okay, but you should drink something. This heat can dehydrate you pretty fast."

Nodding, Gracie rose.

Lord, what's going on? Is Annie telling the truth— or just what she thinks is the truth?

"Troy, I don't get why you don't understand. How can I persuade you to try to get Annie to come back home?" Gracie couldn't keep frustration out of her voice. On her way to LIT after getting off the final bus, she'd stopped at a pay phone and called Troy's cell phone number.

What a waste of time! Why wouldn't he pay attention to her?

"Listen, Gracie, I appreciate how you stepped in to help out with the twins. But this is between me and Annie."

She could hear the sounds of a construction crew behind his voice—hammering, the roar of a distant engine. "I know that. But Annie said some things to me this morning and, meddling or not, I need to know if they're true."

"All right," Troy barked. "What things?"

"Did you really get her pregnant on purpose?"

"No! It just happened. Is that what Annie told you?"

"I think that's what she thinks." The day was suffocating her. Gracie fluffed her hair away from the perspiration on her face.

"Well, she's wrong. And I don't know how she could have gotten that idea."

Gracie didn't know what she should say. What had Annie said—that she'd "overheard" something? These were deep waters and Gracie needed to wade back to firm ground.

"Troy, if you want to get Annie home, you're going to have to convince her that you want her to go ahead and get her education—"

"I've already heard that," he snapped. "From Annie. But I won't be blackmailed into changing what I think just because she's left me. If we have a difference of opinion, she should stay and fight it out."

Gracie couldn't help but agree.

"Things change." A different tone came into Troy's voice. "And people change."

What was it? Was he departing from the truth or did he sense that this was the weak point of his argument? Gracie listened for his next words and their intonation.

"I still think it will be better in the long run if Annie postpones college until she finishes our family by having one more child. And right now—" Troy's voice picked up speed ''—she belongs at home with our kids. When they're in school all day, then she can go to school.''

Gracie listened to Troy, but this time, as her sister might hear these words. *And things change.* If her sister came home today and had another child, would Troy change his mind in a few years and come up with another excuse to keep her home?

''Annie has a lot of anger toward you, Troy,'' Gracie said, choosing her own words with care. ''I think she feels you have been taking her for granted and not really hearing her.''

''Well, I have a lot of anger toward *her* now! *She* left *me.* How do you think that makes me feel?''

Click. Troy had hung up on her.

Gracie hung up, too, and then plodded down the block toward LIT. *Well, Lord, that accomplished exactly nothing. What's wrong with them? Don't they see that this doesn't have to be like this?*

When she could put it off no longer, Gracie walked into the LIT office and looked around for signs of life. The digital wall clock read 11:57. Hearing the tapping of keys from Jack's inner office, she eyed her desk and the flashing red light on the answering machine.

Instead of checking them, she walked to Jack's doorway and leaned against the doorjamb.

As usual, Jack was bent over his computer keyboard. She studied his profile, his intense pose. She recalled how being with the twins had transformed him. It was obvious that he had effortlessly become one of their favorites. She'd never guessed he would be good with children.

"Hi," she said in a quiet voice. Would he ever know that she'd wanted him to be the father of her children?

He went on working.

That was Jack—head stuck in a computer. Brilliant, but clueless. She tried to go back to her desk but she couldn't. They had to talk to one another and make sense of the shifting sands under their feet, the loss of Tom and what that meant.

"Jack?"

He looked up. "Gracie, you didn't come in this morning." He didn't say this as an accusation. Merely as an interesting observation.

She walked over and sat down in the chair beside his desk, stifling the urge to switch off the computer so he could concentrate on her, for a change. "I went to see Annie on campus," she explained.

"Your sister?" His hands left the keys.

She nodded, aware of the attraction she always felt for him. "I wanted to try to persuade her to come home, at least for supper tonight and to visit the twins."

"Did it work?"

His concern for her nephews showed in his eyes. Gracie buried her face in one hand. *This is the way it is and always will be.* Troy wouldn't listen to Annie, and Jack didn't know Gracie was alive.

"Don't cry," Jack said in alarm.

She slid back in her chair and rested her elbows on the arms. "I'm not going to cry. Annie told me that Troy was trying to renege on their agreement that she would go to school this fall."

"I remember he reneged on their original agreement." Jack leaned forward on his elbows. His thick reddish hair was tousled, tempting her to smooth it back.

"Now Annie says Troy was trying to do it again, trying to keep her—" she searched for the word Annie had used "—his 'house-frau.'"

"Maybe he did." Jack stretched his upper body, visibly working out the kinks from sitting so long.

She watched the latent power in his movements and wished for the thousandth time that those arms would claim her.

"I don't know what to believe."

"Hey, is this LIT?" a man's voice called from behind Gracie.

She turned. "Yes, may I—"

The neatly dressed man in his mid-thirties brushed past her. "Are you Jack Lassater?"

Jack rose, staring.

Gracie had never been pushed aside like this before. "*Pardon me,* but Mr. Lassater is busy—"

"Someone who still works at Hope tipped me off. Called me to say you'd been checking up on me—"

"Who are you?" Gracie asked, sliding past the man and allying herself with Jack.

"I'm Dick Witte. I worked for Hope in the finance department until early this year. One of my friends said you were tracking me on the Web—"

"I'm checking out a lot of people," Jack said. "There's no law against it."

"That doesn't mean I have to like it or put up with it. If your intrusion continues, I'll see a lawyer. In fact, several people told me I already have grounds to sue. Dr. Collins didn't let me go according to RIF guidelines, and I can still make trouble."

"Do what you have to do," Jack replied, with no show of emotion. "And I'll do what I have to."

"Fine. But I came here to let you know I'm not going to serve as Hope's scapegoat." The man stomped out.

Jack gave Gracie a quizzical look. "I've just scratched the surface."

Gracie grimaced. And who knows what would pop up next—?

"Hey, it's me!" Tom burst in on them.

Gracie turned her head and silently groaned. *Now they'll want my answer.*

"So have you two thrashed it out?" Tom smiled. "What's your decision?"

She'd known Tom wouldn't beat around the bush.

"I accept your deal." Jack said, cool and decisive. "I'll buy you out with stock and the office setup. Except for my computer."

Feeling as though she'd just swallowed a rock, Gracie tried to read Jack's expression but couldn't.

"Great. I'll have my lawyer draw up—"

"Your lawyer is my lawyer and *I'll* have the agreement drawn up. Just write down what you want," Jack said without any obvious rancor.

Gracie stared at them. How had he come to this decision? Just yesterday he'd acted as if he felt betrayed.

"Okay," Tom agreed. "I'll let you have custody of our lawyer and find new legal counsel for myself."

Then Tom turned his attention to her. "Gracie, I have a few names of businesses that approached us in the month before my vacation, wanting to hire LIT. You can start by following up on them." Tom walked over to his desk, which was uncharacteristically uncluttered.

That alone should have tipped her off that Tom was leaving, Gracie thought morosely.

God, why didn't You warn me?

Tom returned, offering her a few index cards. "Here—"

Gracie looked to Jack. He'd retreated again. When he was with the twins or talking about them, he opened up. She looked to Tom. Why had he suggested she take his position? Was it just a convenient cover for his leaving so abruptly?

Then she recalled her conversation with Troy. Troy couldn't or wouldn't let go of things as they were. *Things change.* She reached for the cards.

"Thanks, Tom." Her voice sounded confident, but her pulse suddenly zoomed to calorie-burn level.

Jack let out a sigh that sounded relieved.

She couldn't look at him. *Feeling as I do, I know I should leave, but I can't.*

"Now, Gracie," Tom said in a conspiratorial tone, "be sure Jack draws up a contract with you, too. You're not just a paltry wage-earner at LIT anymore. You're the sales staff."

"No, I…" Gracie looked around as though seeking guidance.

"He's right." Jack smiled at her.

Her pulse pounded at her temples. Jack's smile lifted her spirits, her hope. They took to the sky on fluttery butterfly wings.

"Though why he thinks I need to be reminded of that, I don't know," Jack concluded.

"Oh, yes, we do, don't we?" Tom teased. "Gracie and I know how your mind *loses* important details."

Gracie didn't trust her voice so she remained silent. Jack had never given her a smile like that before—so personal, so full of understanding.

"Okay, my good man, get your lawyer on this." Tom beamed at them. "My new partner is arriving at the beginning of next week. So you need to vacate within ten days."

"Ten days!" Jack yelped.

Tom gave them a wave as he exited.

Gracie felt like running after him. *Don't go! I changed my mind. I can't do this.*

Jack grimaced and then turned his attention back on her. Directly on her.

She stared back at him.

"You need to hire your replacement," Jack said abruptly.

"Me?"

"Yes, I'm too busy with the Hope project to take time to do that. And you don't have to be in a big hurry to drum us up another client. First of all, we'll need clerical staff and a new place to work. That's what you should concentrate on."

"Is that all?" Gracie asked, resting her hands on her hips.

"Yeah." He turned back to the computer. "Call our lawyer, too. And tell him to expect to be writing up new contracts with Tom and one with you."

"Jack, just because I've agreed to try my hand at sales," she cautioned, "doesn't mean that I'm going to handle everything."

"I'm right in the middle of designing a new encryption for Hope and then I'm going forward with the design of a whole new security protocol for them. I've also been following up all their leads and keeping a finger on Dr. Collins." He tapped away, picking up speed. "I can't be bothered with anything else right now. You can do what's necessary. You've never failed me before."

Warmed by his unlooked-for praise, Gracie acknowledged defeat and rose.

"Oh." Jack's voice sounded funny. "We should

do something to celebrate your moving up to marketing and sales. Make reservations for us for dinner tonight. Somewhere with thick steaks. I'm going to be hungry.''

The three of them—Jack, Tom and Gracie—had often gone out casually after work or to celebrate a new contract on the spur of the moment. But reservations? Jack had never told her to do that before.

''That's not necessary.''

''Yes, it is. Don't you think I know how big a favor you're doing me?'' Then he officially tuned out.

She recognized the symptoms, his intent expression, his hands moving over the keyboard.

Jack was taking her to dinner, just her. A warm glow spread through her, lifting the corners of her mouth into what she thought must be a goofy smile.

Gracie tapped on Jack's door. The blue sky outside was darkening into lavender twilight.

Jack didn't look up.

''Jack, it's time to quit.''

He looked up then. ''What time is it?''

''Nearly eight. We have reservations at Sharkey's in a half hour.'' Gracie folded her hands and waited to see what he would say.

''Reservations?''

''You told me to make reservations for—''

''For a thick steak dinner to celebrate your promotion,'' he finished. ''I didn't forget and I'm starved.''

He closed the files and shut down his computer. ''Let's go.''

The phone rang on Gracie's desk. She went to it. ''LIT, Gracie Petrov speaking.''

''Gracie, it's Cliff Lassater. I need to talk to Jack—stat.''

Chapter Seven

"Here comes your father," Gracie murmured, looking over her shoulder.

Sitting across from her in a booth at Sharkey's, Jack observed his father approaching. Ignoring the waiter following him, Cliff was walking fast and frowning.

When they'd arrived at Sharkey's, Gracie had slipped off her blazer and unbuttoned the top button of her sleeveless blouse. In the low light of the restaurant, the thin string of pearls glowed against her pale neck.

Arriving, Cliff slid in beside Gracie and turned down the menu offered by a waiter, waving the man away. "Our payroll has been corrupted."

Jack whispered a curse. He also resented his father's disrupting his meal with Gracie. Couldn't they even have a moment of celebration without his dad bursting in?

"What have you accomplished so far?" Cliff demanded. "How did this happen?"

Jack stared at his dad. "Get real. I've only been on the job a few days. Your system's security was Stone Age. For the past few years, you've been a sitting duck and didn't even know it. Why didn't anyone think to keep up with new security?"

Cliff grimaced. "You're saying this is our own fault?"

Jack nodded, his gaze not leaving his dad's face.

"Perhaps...you've been complacent," Gracie suggested in a subdued tone. "You didn't think anyone would have a motive to interrupt your system."

Both men turned to her.

That was just like Gracie. She was too kind. Her delicate hand rested on the table. Jack stretched out his next to hers. *Be careful not to touch her.*

Cliff rewarded Gracie's tact with a half smile. "I guess we're not computer types. Most of us are too involved in our practices and patients.... Just keeping up with the innovations in our own fields keeps us buried."

The waiter arrived at the table and served Gracie and Jack their steaks sizzling on metal plates. The delicious aroma of charcoal-broiled beef made Jack's empty stomach rumble.

"You need to hire a full-time computer person—" Jack picked up his knife and fork "—who would be responsible for your programs and security. I've started designing a new encryption code for Hope. But it will take me some time to finish it and then I'll have to update all your passwords. What exactly did the hacker do to your payroll?''

''Wildly inflated checks.'' His dad waved toward Gracie's plate, encouraging her to go ahead and begin eating. ''We had to stop payment on them—that will cost a pretty penny—and hire an outside firm to issue a whole new payroll. Our employees are up in arms about the delay.''

Jack sliced his first bite of rare steak and bit into it. ''Couldn't this have waited till tomorrow morning? I can't do anything about what's happening to your outdated, compromised system.''

''Those who have their checks direct-deposited and for whom we've delayed the deposits,'' his dad continued, ignoring his question, ''also had automatic withdrawals which will come back as delinquent with insufficient-funds charges.'' Cliff rubbed his hand over his forehead. ''It's been a nightmare. Our employees and the custodial and other unions are screaming for somebody's blood.''

''They'll calm down,'' Gracie said in a soothing tone. ''When the new checks arrive and you agree to pay for all delinquent charges for returned checks, et cetera.''

Cliff looked sideways at her. ''I suppose that's what we'll have to do.'' Then he glanced across at

Jack. "When will the new encryption be ready to go?"

"Soon." Jack cut another bite of the succulent Iowa corn-fed beef Sharkey's was noted for. "I do encryption all the time. That's not the problem."

"Then, what *is* the problem?" Cliff barked.

Jack made eye contact with his father. "I told you before. The problem is who is doing this and why. Your Board has started on a list of possible suspects, people with grudges against Hope. I'm keeping tabs on the very unhappy Dr. Collins—just in case—and today, Dick Witte burst into my office and threatened a lawsuit because I was checking him out. Finding the culprit is really the key here."

Cliff frowned. "Is that necessary? I mean, if you put the new security in place, won't that stop whoever it is?"

"For a while." Jack watched Gracie adding butter and sour cream to her baked potato. She was always so precise about everything she did. Like the golden butter melting on her plate, he felt himself soften toward her.

"But I also told you, no program is invincible," he continued. "I can tighten your security. But I can't guarantee that it can never again be breached, even with regular updates. If someone is out to get you and is really clever, he will break in eventually."

"That is not what I wanted to hear." Cliff rose.

"I warned you at the pool party of my limitations." *I didn't want to take on your project. I only*

*did it to help Mom, to make it your money that would
pay for her addition. And now she doesn't want my
money.*

"I have to go home and call the Board. We'll have
to get a meeting together and continue working on
that suspect list." Cliff started to walk away and then
stopped to address Gracie. "Good night. Sorry to
have disturbed your dinner." He left as he had
come—quickly and gloomily.

"Were you able to find out anything about the
hacker?" Gracie asked Jack.

"He's smart, almost brilliant. But what really wor-
ries me is that no matter what my father just said,
the Board still hasn't taken finding the hacker seri-
ously. They are treating it like a natural disaster.
They just wanted me to clean up the mess so they
could get back to business as usual."

Gracie gazed at him. Jack studied her eyes. They
were more round than oval and they looked luminous
in the candlelight.

"You mean that you think the hacker will strike
again?" She finally cut into her steak.

"'Strike' is a flamboyant word. But yes, this isn't
over. Not until we catch him or her."

Nearly a week later, Gracie's nerve endings zinged
with tension. Jack stood beside her, stolid and silent.
*I can't believe I thought this would be a good place
for us to move LIT.*

Mama Kalanovski unlocked the door to the vacant

storefront next to the Polska Café. "This ain't a classy address," Mama said over her shoulder to Jack.

"Gracie already explained that to me," Jack said, looking at ease in tan chinos and a clay-colored knit shirt, one that matched the red in his hair.

"I could have looked downtown," Gracie mentioned, but was ignored. *Jack doesn't belong here.* The contrast between Jack and the working-class setting was striking. *I don't even have Tom there to run interference between us. I play with fire every day I show up for work.*

"And it's been vacant for over a year," Mama continued.

"Gracie said it would need some work." Jack looked up and down the street.

"Yeah, a good cleaning wouldn't hurt." Mama chuckled.

Gracie cringed. Jack's father had thought he was slumming when they'd merely lunched next door. Jack must have agreed because he thought it was a good joke on his father.

Gracie almost wished he wouldn't be so polite for her sake. *He should just have said no.*

"Okay," Mama said. "I just don't want you to be insulted. This ain't Michigan Avenue." She opened the door and waved them inside.

Touching her shoulder, Jack let Gracie precede him.

"When you're done, lock up and bring me the key." Entrusting it to Gracie, she left them.

With a feeling of fatalism, Grace switched on the high fluorescent lights. She and Jack had stirred up dust when they'd entered. It danced in the light, swirling like her nerves.

"I know it doesn't look like much," she mumbled.

Jack scanned the bare room. His expression told her little.

He'll hate it. She glanced at shelves from the previous owner, partially dismantled, some lying on the floor and the rest propped against the far wall. She contrasted this with the sleek office they'd just vacated.

"This probably wasn't what you were visualizing as new office space for us," she said in a halfhearted tone, feeling very much that she'd dropped the ball. "But it's really reasonable, and Mama said she and her husband would pay for paint and all, if we wanted to update it ourselves."

Jack nodded, turning in a slow circle as he inspected the large open room.

Why didn't he react? It was spooky. *Just tell me you hate it, Jack, and we'll leave.*

"What's in the back?" Jack walked toward the rear entrance, but kept glancing at her.

"A little kitchen, kind of a break area or a stock area." Why did he keep looking at her? She followed him, hope trembling to life.

He waited for her to catch up. "What was this before?"

"A hardware store." She kept pace with him now. "But the owner passed away and the Kalanovskis bought it from the heirs because they wanted to control what kind of business moved in beside them."

Jack inclined his ear as though hanging on her every word.

Gracie watched Jack assessing the space. "A man who wanted to put in an adult entertainment store here had approached the heirs."

His gaze unnerved her, but she went on. "The Kalanovskis thought that kind of store would ruin our solid family neighborhood."

"I see." Jack flipped on the light switch in the back room and gazed around, his expression still unreadable. But he remained close at her side.

"If we rented from the Kalanovskis, it would be trouble-free." She felt herself beginning to babble. Jack's obvious deference to her judgment and his close attention was unnerving. "They're honest people. Our neighborhood has low crime. Everyone watches out for each other...."

He nodded, but stared at her, not the empty store. Did she have a smudge on her nose or something? What was going on? She couldn't stand the tension anymore.

"So what do you think?"

"Well, the rent is more than reasonable."

She took a deep, calming breath. "I thought while

we're making a change like this, it would be best to keep our expenses low. But we would have to put in some sweat equity. My dad said he'd help us whip it into shape this weekend.''

Still only inches from her, he nodded.

Even under his eye, her confidence flickered brighter. ''And there is a postal station not far from here where we can rent a large post box so our customers wouldn't have to ever know our address.''

''I'm not worried about impressing people. Hewlett and Packard started in a garage, remember?'' Taking a step from her, he peered out of the high small window in the alley door.

She hovered near him. ''Well, this is definitely a step up from a garage,'' she said with an attempt at humor. ''And I've already chosen a downtown restaurant where I can meet with prospective clients.''

''Well, you sound like you've thought of everything.''

''I tried to.'' *So, Jack?* She took a step closer.

He turned toward her, his nose just missing hers.

She froze. The inches between them became charged, vital.

Jack, why are you so different today? Gracie looked into his blue eyes and leaned closer.

Responding, he slanted forward and pressed his lips to hers.

Gracie closed her eyes, savoring the contact she'd dreamed of for so long, his lips on hers. Jack...

"Hi, kids!" Voices summoned them from the front. The door banged shut.

Gracie and Jack stumbled apart and whirled toward the voices. Through the doorway, she glimpsed her dad and Sandy.

"Hi, Gracie. Mama said you were here." Mike beamed at them.

Gracie felt her cheeks flaming, as though they were a flashing neon-orange sign repeating, "I Kissed Jack! Jack Kissed Me!"

"Mom, I didn't expect to see you here," Jack blurted out.

Gracie breathed steadily in and out, willing away the guilty stain she could feel on her cheeks. Would her dad notice her blushes? Had they glimpsed Jack kissing her?

"Look, I'm off my crutches." Sandy motioned grandly. "Mike invited me to lunch at the Polska to celebrate."

Gracie eyed Jack with uncertainty. Was he disgruntled, grumpy? What was the matter with him?

"That's great!" Gracie enthused, to cover Jack's obvious displeasure and her discomfiture. Her lips still tingled after Jack's kiss.

"We've just been to a store to pick out flooring, paint and wallpaper for my addition." Sandy looked around the large room.

"That's what we'll be doing soon," Gracie hurried to say, still covering Jack's silence. "We're going to rent this for LIT."

"Wonderful," Mike said. "You'll be right in the neighborhood." Then he put an arm around Sandy's shoulders.

Jack folded his arms and glared at Mike.

Oh dear. Gracie hoped she was wrong about what was upsetting Jack.

A day later, at Cliff's invitation, Gracie and Jack stood in line at the dinner buffet in a suburban country club, overlooking the groomed, brilliant-green golf course. He and Gracie had parted immediately after his approving her decision to rent the place next to the Polska. *And right after I gave into crazy temptation and kissed her.*

Why did I kiss Gracie? What was I thinking? I'm lucky she didn't quit right then.

Jack watched the casually but expensively dressed people milling around them and the ones who'd gotten in line after them. But his mind was divided between the present and what had happened the day before. The kiss. *She did kiss me back. What did that mean?*

"Why are we here?" Gracie whispered to him. "I keep asking and you won't tell me."

Her whisper made the hair on the back of his neck whisker up. He hesitated, getting control of his voice. "I want to get a better feel for the Board members." He added silently, *I suspect that someone here has an enemy. Since I haven't located the hacker, maybe I can find out who his target is.*

So far though, except for Gracie's undiluted presence, which acted on him like a stimulant, Jack had only been bored to death. No wonder these people had to anesthetize themselves with a cocktail hour before dinner. Why did people think hitting a little ball into eighteen holes was of universal and intense interest?

"Are you sure you're not doing some amateur sleuthing?" she whispered.

"Keep that to yourself." Jack suddenly recalled how soft her lips had been. They'd just been alone at the new storefront and, without warning, she'd become an irresistible force to him, his North Star. *Why?*

"What do you expect to find out?" Gracie scooped salad greens generously onto her plate.

"I don't know. Maybe just get a second impression of Dr. Collins."

Neither he nor Gracie had said one word about that kiss. He'd been afraid of how she might respond if he did. *I guess it didn't shake her up like it did me— fortunately.* He tried to feel fortunate, but failed.

The two of them reached the end of the line. "Where do you want to sit?" she asked.

Dr. Collins was seated at a table to Jack's far right.

Jack was gazing around when another thought came. Should he apologize to her for kissing her? *I just won't let it happen again. I've lost Tom. I can't afford to lose Gracie.*

A woman stood and flicked her hand, beckoning them.

Jack recognized her as Mrs. Dunn, the woman who'd hosted the pool party he and Gracie had attended. Jack nudged Gracie to head toward them. Then they would be sitting at the table beside Collins.

Dunn and his svelte wife sat at a round table in the corner of the room. "We were pleased when you accepted our invitation to come tonight," the wife said. "Your father said you usually don't like to mix business and pleasure."

"Maybe this isn't pleasure." The husband spoke up, an edge to his voice. "Maybe he's come to ruin our meal with questions."

Jack lifted an eyebrow. Out of the corner of his eye, he noted Dr. Collins watching and listening.

"Cliff made it clear that you think we aren't doing enough to assist you." Dunn buttered his roll with a vengeance.

Jack set his plate down and pulled out a chair for Gracie. Ignoring the man's challenge, he found himself contrasting Mrs. Dunn and Gracie.

He didn't like the look of the pencil-thin surgeon's wife—too much makeup and too much jewelry. In his opinion, Gracie, with her unaffected hairstyle and sprinkle of freckles over her nose, won hands down.

"Well?" Dunn pushed for an answer.

"I've been getting many leads, but so far none has panned out. I suspect that someone on the Board is being targeted." Jack finished seating Gracie and then sat down, too. "Maybe you could give me a few suggestions of who that might be."

"Is that possible?" Dunn asked. "We aren't in the business of hurting people. We spend our days repairing broken and diseased bodies—"

"Hackers are not the most logical people." Jack turned away from Gracie, trying to ignore the subtle Gracie fragrance he'd become aware of so intensely that night in his mother's kitchen.

"What does that mean?" Dunn fixed his gaze on Jack.

Jack glanced around, seeking his dad. Cliff was at another table, but within hearing distance. "It means that the hacker's motive might not be obvious or even sensible."

"I didn't think of that." Dunn looked as if he were giving that some thought.

Gracie nibbled her salad, but Jack sensed her close attention to the exchange. He dragged his mind back to the subject at hand. "Has Hope had to let any troublesome employees go in the past year?"

Dunn pursed his lips. "Cliff asked that question right after we met you at our pool party. I can't think of anyone we've let go—"

"What about that nurse who was trying to unionize the nursing staff at Highland Hills Hospital?" Dr. Brown, tall but unprepossessing, sat down with her husband beside her.

"We didn't fire her," Dunn objected. "She had

every right to try to organize the nursing staff and the staff had every right to vote it down.''

Jack watched Gracie butter a roll, fascinated by the adroit action of her fingers. Everything about Gracie looked fragile. But she wasn't. She was strong—like his mother.

''Did you put any pressure on the staff not to vote themselves into a union?''

''Trying to prevent unionization is illegal,'' Dunn said. ''We didn't think the nurses needed to unionize, but we did nothing to stop it.''

''Is this part of your job?'' Dr. Brown asked, sitting forward in her chair. ''To try to track down the hacker?''

''Yes,'' Jack replied. ''LIT has been hired to fix and secure your system. But after this latest episode, I warned my father that no system is impregnable. Mitnik invaded the government's databases before he was finally tracked down.''

''Was that the notorious hacker that was imprisoned in the nineties?'' Brown asked.

''Yes.'' Jack nodded. ''I don't think your hacker is in that league. What does someone want to gain by messing up your payroll and your insurance data? We need to consider motive.''

No one replied.

Jack noted Dr. Collins turn quietly away from them after obviously taking in all that had been said.

''Let's change subjects. All this business talk is spoiling my dinner.'' Mrs. Dunn looked at Jack. ''So, what do you think of Gloria?'' Mrs. Dunn took a sip of her water.

"Gloria?" Jack looked to Gracie for information. Had he met a Gloria?

Gracie responded with a small shake of her head.

"Was that the nurse who wanted to unionize?" Jack asked.

"No! She's your father's fiancée." The woman watched him, looking pleased, as though she had scored a point in some game she was playing.

Jack said nothing.

"We haven't had the pleasure of meeting her yet," Gracie said, filling the gap for him.

"That's right." Cliff, who'd finally decided to come over from his table, sat down beside Jack. "Gloria has been away with a few family emergencies since I proposed."

Jack managed to nod.

"I'm hoping they'll get to meet her when she gets home in the coming month." Cliff looked to Jack as though daring him to say something negative.

Gracie's cell phone made a subtle buzzing sound and she took it out of her pocket. She turned to Jack as she listened.

"I can't believe that," she said into the small phone. Pause. "Okay. I'll be home as soon as I can." She slid the phone back into her pocket.

"What was it?" Jack murmured into her ear.

"Later." Her tone was curt.

Chapter Eight

Gracie chewed her lower lip as Jack parked in front of her house. "Thanks for bringing me home early." She reached for the door handle, eager to get away from him.

"Hold it. It's late. I'm walking you in." He released his seat belt. It slithered into its holder.

"No." She gripped the handle. *I don't know what we'll find inside, Jack, and I don't want you to see my family this way.*

"You've been upset since you got that phone call—"

Her phone buzzed again. *What now?* She lifted it from her pocket. "Hi."

Gracie, I need you at home," her dad urged. "Now."

"I'm in front of the house. I'll be right in." At

her father's anxious voice, her pulse raced. She felt a little sick as she hung up. "I've got to go."

"I'm coming with—"

"No, I..." *Please, Jack, don't. This is too personal.*

Unfazed, he climbed out, zipped around and met her at the curb. "What is it?"

Under the bronzed sky, she shook her head, unable to put her hesitance into words. She headed for her front gate.

But Jack kept up with her.

As she unlocked the front door and hurried inside, he doggedly followed her into the foyer.

Raised male voices greeted them.

Gracie rushed into the first-floor flat. In the living room, Mike and Troy faced one another. Their hostile expressions—so out of character—made the hair on her nape stand up.

"I'm not standing for this!" Troy shouted.

Her dad's hair was mussed and tension stiffened his posture. Stress showed in the way he edged forward, confronting Troy. "I called Annie immediately after this arrived for you. She said she'd come as soon as she could. She's on her way. Why won't you agree to talk this over with her?"

"She's gone too far." Troy shook a sheaf of papers in Mike's face. "And *I* don't want to talk to *her.*"

"She said she'd be right over—" Mike insisted, reaching for Troy's arm.

The front door opened. Annie walked in.

Gracie took a step forward.

"You!" Troy's voice was accusing.

"Yes, me. Dad called and I came." Annie tossed a defiant glare at her husband.

Gracie froze where she was, unable to believe what was happening around her. *Lord, it's worse than I thought. Help us.*

Troy waved the document in Annie's face. "You've gone too far—"

"Really?" Annie lifted her chin. "I think it was the *very least* I could do in the situation *you* put us in—"

"Me?" Troy glared. "*I* didn't walk out."

Her head cocked, Annie folded her arms in front of her. "I was forced out. It was your way or the highway."

Oh, Annie! Gracie turned to Jack. "We should go and let them—"

"I," Troy yelled, "never said that—"

"Stop this!" Mike roared.

Silence.

Gracie realized Jack had moved to her side. She put out a hand. He took it and she clung to him.

"This is not the kind of home where family members yell at one another." Mike looked at Annie and then Troy. "Now, we're going to sit down and discuss this like a family."

"Yes, listen to Dad," Gracie coaxed.

"I'm not discussing anything here." Troy folded

his arms. "You'll take her side. She's your daughter."

Mike stared at him as though he couldn't believe what Troy had just uttered. "I won't be doing any of the talking. You two will—"

Troy swung away toward the front door. "I'm leaving. Ann Marie, you'll be hearing from my lawyer—"

Suddenly, before Gracie's horrified gaze, two little boys appeared in the kitchen doorway. Austin and Andy rubbed their sleepy eyes. Then Austin did a hop. "Mommy!" he crowed.

"Go back to bed." Troy warned them.

Ignoring their father, the two of them, both squealing, stormed their mother and wrapped themselves around her legs.

Annie bent over, hugging them back, murmuring a broken, teary greeting.

"Mommy's home! Mommy's home!" The twins danced and jumped around her, but without letting go.

Lord, protect these little ones, Gracie prayed silently, as she edged closer to the boys.

Jack stayed at her side. Suddenly, she realized she was glad he was here—his presence bolstered her.

Troy glared at Annie, whose eyes now glistened with unshed tears. "You boys have to go back up to bed," he insisted.

"But Mommy's here!" Austin declared as though their father were blind.

"Not for long," Troy started. "She doesn't care about you—"

Jack lunged at Troy, grabbing the front of his shirt. "That's enough," he hissed. "Don't use your kids like that."

Gracie gasped.

Red-faced, Troy sputtered, shocked. He grasped Jack's hand.

"No! Don't, Troy!" Gracie rose onto the balls of her feet, ready to come between the two men who stood nose to nose. *This isn't happening.*

An uneasy silence hung over them all.

Gracie realized she'd stopped breathing, and drew in air.

Austin and Andy retained their hold on the denim of their mother's jean shorts. "Mr. Lassater, don't hurt our daddy," Andy implored.

Gracie ached for him as Andy's lower lip trembled.

Jack let go of Troy's shirt. "I won't."

Troy muttered under his breath, still glowering at Jack.

"I think," Jack said in a calm tone, "Gracie and I will take the boys upstairs." He glanced over his shoulder at her. "Shall we help them get settled down again for the night?"

"I think that's an excellent idea." Mike spoke up, moving to stand by Jack.

"But we don't want Mommy to leave," Austin said. Neither boy released his death grip on Annie.

"Your mother will be here in the morning." Mike bent down to look them in the eyes. "I promise."

"But we want her now," Andy objected, nearly whining.

"Don't go, Mommy," Austin pleaded.

Gracie's throat clogged with swallowed tears.

Mike made eye contact with each twin. "Your mommy and daddy need to sit down and talk things through so we can settle when Mommy is coming home for good."

Troy's face flushed with anger. "I won't be manipulated."

"Neither will I," Annie muttered.

Mike rose, giving both his daughter and his son-in-law a warning glance.

"No one will be manipulated," Gracie said, finally able to speak.

"And *no one* will be able to disturb *others*," Jack asserted with a significant nod at the twins. Turning toward the boys, he squatted and opened his arms. "Guys, kiss your mommy good-night and come with me and your aunt. You will see your mommy here in the morning. I promise."

The twins gazed up at their mother. The question *Will you be here in the morning?* was plain in their identical expressions.

Annie bent her knees and again gathered them into her arms. "I'll be here in the morning, guys. And I'll make you sausages and pancakes with raisin smiles, just the way you like."

This worked. Each twin took a turn hugging her neck and smooching her. Then they rushed Jack.

One in each arm, he rose. "Come on, Aunt Gracie, let's get these boys back to bed."

Gracie led him through the kitchen and motioned him up the back stairs. Cool relief whistled through her. She closed the door behind her, so the twins wouldn't hear any more acrimony. Jack's quick action had shocked her, but it had stopped Troy from doing any more damage.

Dear Lord, help us. Help my dad downstairs.

In the upper level, Jack let the boys lead, his hands in theirs, to their room. They pushed him toward a large rocker in one corner of the room.

Jack allowed this. As soon as his seat touched the chair, both boys claimed a portion of his lap. "Read us a story," they begged in unison.

Jack looked to her, asking her silently what to do.

Why did he look so natural doing this, caring about the boys and trying to help? *It isn't fair—it makes me love him all the more.* But she nodded her approval and then trusted her voice.

"I think that's a good idea. Why don't each of you pick out a book for Mr. Lassater to read you?"

While the twins scrambled to choose their favorite books, Gracie smoothed the purple sheets and thin summer bedspreads on their twin beds. Anything, just so she could put some distance, a buffer between Jack and her. The memory of their kiss remained always just below the surface, tempting her to believe Jack might someday soon wake up and notice her.

And this setting was dangerous. Being here with Jack was only a short step from imagining that she and Jack were the mother and father and she was doing this for their sons. Or maybe daughters?

It didn't help that she'd let herself draw closer to Jack when she'd known she should have drawn away. She'd been weak or sentimental enough to let it happen, and that did nothing to improve the situation. Or make it look more promising.

Without Tom at LIT, she must stay with Jack until he got his feet under him. She couldn't resign. But spending her days with him was becoming more and more of a severe test. And more than ever before, they were being thrown together over and over without the distraction of a third party.

And renting that storefront so close to home had been a big mistake. It would make it more and more difficult to break with Jack.

"What's wrong, Aunty?" Austin asked.

She looked up. "Nothing's wrong. Why?"

"You look like Mommy does when she says she has a headache." Andy ran across the short distance and hugged her neck. Austin followed.

Oh, Lord, protect these children and keep their family together.

She hugged and kissed both twins. And then she led them back to Jack. They climbed onto his lap. His unique scent—aftershave or soap, and Jack himself—filled her head. She moved away, fearful of letting her response to him show.

Jack opened the first book and began reading *Green Eggs and Ham.* He caught on to Dr. Seuss's rhythmic verses, and before long had the twins smiling again. Then he closed that book, laid it down on the foot of the nearest bed and opened the final book, *Tell Me a Story.*

Gracie sat down on the side of Andy's bed, facing Jack. But she tried not to react to his story reading. Another talent she'd never guessed he possessed.

Jack's voice became quieter and lower as he went through the story of different animal babies who asked their mothers to ''tell me a story'' and then, as the mother read to each, the baby animal fell asleep.

Gracie blinked as his soothing voice increased her languor, making her eyelids heavy. With a yawn, she gave in and lay down on the bed, trying not to imagine Jack lying beside her with an arm around her.

Jack droned on, ''And the baby fox said to his mother, 'Tell me a story...'''

She closed her eyes, letting his deep, even voice flow over her. The cotton sheet was cool and soft against her cheek. *Jack can take care of the boys....*

''Gracie,'' Jack whispered. ''Gracie?''

She opened her eyes and realized that she had almost fallen asleep. ''Jack,'' she whispered back, ''why are we whispering?''

"I need you to help me," he said. "I don't want to wake them."

Enmeshed in her own drowsiness, she made herself sit up and look at him more closely. Both twins had fallen asleep in his arms. One white-blond head lolled over each arm.

Rising, she tiptoed over and drew Andy into her arms. She carried his small, completely relaxed warm body to bed and laid him down. She kissed his cheek and whispered, "Sweet dreams."

Andy squirmed into his pillow but did not waken.

Jack followed her lead and did the same with Austin, including an awkward kiss and the same phrase.

Once again, seeing Jack caring for a child touched her heart.

Trying not to show this, she led him out into Troy and Annie's living room. She looked around, remembering helping Annie, a new bride, pick out the gleaming white paint and Victorian roses wallpaper for the room. "I thought Annie was the luckiest girl in the world."

"Pardon?" Jack spoke at her elbow.

His voice made her shiver. "Nothing." She turned and smiled tentatively at him. "Thanks. You're great with the boys."

He said in a gruff tone, "I hope those two downstairs don't act up like that again in front of their boys. They don't deserve two great kids if they're going to throw tantrums like that." Jack looked grim. "What triggered this?"

She led him to the nearby couch and sat down. "Dad called me while we were at the county club to tell me that Annie had Troy served with separate maintenance papers today."

"Separate maintenance?" Jack sat down beside her, making the sofa dip.

"She had a lawyer contact Troy to set up an agreement for them to live apart." Gracie hated having to tell him this.

"Isn't that like a pre-divorce or something?" Jack wrinkled his nose.

"I don't know, but I do think I know why she did it."

"Why?" He leaned forward, resting his elbows on his thighs.

Again, his clean-soap scent filled her senses. "Troy said she couldn't see the boys. I'm pretty sure that the separate maintenance agreement would force Troy to let her have visitation rights on a regular basis."

"You think that was her motivation?"

Resisting the urge to smooth back his hair, Gracie nodded.

"That wasn't a pretty scene downstairs." His voice betrayed just how intensely Annie and Troy had upset him.

"No, it wasn't." Gracie watched him, wondering if Sandy and Cliff had enacted any such scenes in front of him.

"I hope the two of them wake up or grow up

before they end up hurting their kids,'' Jack said, repeating what was obviously his main concern.

And it touched her heart. She could only nod.

They heard hasty footsteps on the back stairs. Gracie rose and so did Jack. Together, they faced Troy as he entered the room.

''You two can go now,'' Troy said in a sullen tone.

Gracie nearly asked, *How did it go?* But Troy's demeanor spoke volumes. ''The boys are asleep. Good night, brother-in-law.''

''Good night.'' Troy stalked past them to his bedroom.

Gracie and Jack exchanged looks and headed toward the front stairs. Gracie wanted to show Jack out before she faced her sister and dad downstairs.

At the front door, Jack paused. ''I'll say a prayer for you and your family. Good night.'' He leaned forward as if to kiss her again.

That kiss, that wonderful, disturbing kiss. She looked into his eyes and saw the sympathy, concern and the desire to stay. With her? She hardened herself against them all.

''Good night, Jack. See you tomorrow.''

On Saturday morning, Jack watched Gracie painstakingly press the masking tape along the window frame. She'd called him yesterday and suggested they paint their new office. He wanted to tell her his good news, but doing that in this setting didn't seem appropriate. Or was it his new heightened awareness of Gracie that made it difficult to start a conversation? Or was it that he had kissed her here just days ago?

Why had he begun to discern things about Gracie he'd never noticed before? "I've never done much painting," he muttered.

"Goodness! We're not ready to paint yet." Gracie gave him a tart look.

He noted again the faint freckles dotting her nose. *Why am I noticing Gracie's freckles?* "Then, what are we doing?" He tried to work up some enthusiasm for this, but couldn't. He'd much rather stand and stare at his new sales manager.

"We need to move the shelves out to the alley for disposal and then sweep the floors. Then we can scrub the walls and Spackle the nicks and cracks."

Even this list of unappealing chores didn't dull his new and very keen concentration on Gracie Petrov. "That's all I need to know now," Jack said. "Thanks. Are you sure we couldn't just hire this done?" *Gracie shouldn't have to do this kind of stuff.*

"This little bit of work?" Gracie said, scanning the dilapidated-looking store. "The bottom line is the bottom line, Jack. We need to be careful of it while we're—you're—buying Tom out."

Jack couldn't argue with that. But he almost said, *while we're buying Tom out is the right way to say that.* LIT wouldn't be LIT without Gracie.

Now why had that popped into his head? Was it

because he'd had to let Tom leave to follow his dream? Would Gracie decide to leave him, too, someday? Something Tom had said about Jack proposing to Gracie replayed in Jack's mind. *What an odd thing for Tom to say.*

"Besides, help is expected later." Gracie turned back to the window. "It won't take long for us to get this place ready to paint. And the painting will go fast."

He wanted to ask her about her sister's situation, but didn't know how to bring that up, either.

"Where's the broom?" he asked instead.

"In the back room, and I rented a Dumpster for us. It's in the alley." Gracie was back to concentrating on masking the window.

"Okay, boss." Jack saluted her.

In the back room, he located the new broom and dustpan and peered out the door at the bright green Dumpster in the narrow alley. Leave it to Gracie to think of a Dumpster. Then he returned to the large room and began to lift the first piece of shelving. The metal groaned and grated against the aged, painted hardwood floor.

"Wait." Gracie swung again. "I'll help you with that. It will go quicker and do less damage to the floor if we work together."

"This is heavy."

Gracie lifted her end. "They're more unwieldy than heavy."

Jack couldn't argue with her—at least, not while

walking backward, clumsily carrying a hunk of metal...and watching Gracie's shapely legs.

With her upper body hidden by the bulky shelf, he found he could finally tell Gracie the good news. "I finished last night," he said to his unseen sales partner.

"Finished?" Gracie, still unseen, asked.

"Yes, late last night, I finished the software update in record time—" he backed through the door to the rear area "—and issued new passwords to Hope Medical Group."

"That's great, Jack! Was your dad pleased?"

"I don't know. I just e-mailed him the news and sent the new passwords via sealed office memos from their central office." Jack pushed the rear door open with his back and entered the alley.

"I'm relieved. In the back of my mind, I was worried about a hacker messing around with patient files. That would be scary." She looked around the shelf and nodded toward the Dumpster behind him. "Just a little farther," she murmured.

"Well, the medical files were never accessed by the hacker—just the financial accounts." He set his end of the shelf down, opened the lid, and with Gracie's help managed to heft the shelf into the Dumpster.

"I know, but it still bothered—"

"Hi, we're here!" A female voice from inside the store summoned Jack and Gracie in from the alley.

"Patience! Connie!" Gracie greeted a pretty

blonde and an equally pretty brunette, both dressed in faded jeans and shirts, waiting in the back room. "Jack, you remember my cousin, Patience Andrews?" She motioned toward the blonde.

"Sure." She did look familiar. A little. He shook hands with her.

"And this is Connie Oberlin, an old friend from here in the neighborhood."

"Patience, you recall," Gracie announced with obvious pride, "just graduated with her education degree with honors and is looking for a fall teaching job."

He nodded. *Okay, where's this leading?*

"And Connie is in law school," Gracie said with identical pride.

"Hi, Jack." Connie, the brunette, held out her hand to him.

He shook it politely.

"Did you ask him yet?" Patience asked.

"No—"

Gracie turned to him, her expression brimming with…excitement?

"Contingent on your approval, of course, I've hired Patience to do our clerical work part-time."

"Don't we need someone full-time?" he asked.

"I've also hired Connie part-time." Gracie looked at him expectantly.

"Yes, so the two of us together make one whole employee," Connie said with a grin.

"Is that all right?" Gracie looked up at him with doubt. "Things have been so hectic—"

Jack swallowed. Gracie wore a delicate gold chain around her neck, and for some reason, it called for his attention. He made himself look at Connie and Patience and tried to figure out why their arrival felt like an intrusion.

"It's fine, great."

"And we're here today to help—gratis," Patience added. "What do you want us to do?"

"We need to move this old shelving out and clean up." Gracie grinned. "Then the painting begins!"

For the first few minutes, the four of them, in teams of two—he and Gracie and the two young women—"wobbled" the shelves out to the alley and deposited them into the Dumpster.

While Gracie masking-taped the large front windows, standing on an old ladder that came with the store, Patience began washing down the walls with a sponge mop and Connie started cleaning the small kitchen area in the back room.

Jack began sweeping the floor in the main room and tried hard not to keep looking at Gracie. *What is going on with me?* He couldn't figure out why, but it was as though an invisible thread connected him to Gracie. She couldn't make the slightest move without his being aware of it.

Thoughts of Dr. Collins and Dick Witte kept rolling around in Jack's mind. He'd verified that both of them had the knowledge of computers to qualify as suspects. But he hadn't connected either with what had happened at Hope—yet.

"Gracie," Patience asked over her shoulder, "what's the latest on Annie and Troy?"

Jack listened intently.

Connie spoke up before Gracie replied. "Earlier this week Troy called me to ask about the separate maintenance papers he was served with. What's that all about?"

Gracie turned on the ladder to face them. "Annie has agreed to put that on hold," Gracie replied, "as long as she can visit the twins in the evenings and on weekends when she's free."

Jack didn't like the worry in Gracie's voice. Why couldn't Annie just settle things with her husband? On the other hand, Troy hadn't acted like a reasonable man the other night.

"I just don't get this," Connie said from the back room. "When Troy called me, he didn't even sound like himself."

"It's been pretty tense," Patience agreed, swabbing the wall with long strokes.

"I tried to talk to Annie and she was…angry," Connie added. "I've never seen her act like that either."

"Divorce brings out the worst in people," Jack muttered.

"Hello!" A voice from the front door greeted them.

Jack turned...to see his mom and Mike Petrov walk in together.

"We came to give you a hand." Sandy beamed.

Jack frowned at Mike, who was resting his hand on Mom's shoulder.

He studied the screen and tried not to feel... stupid. That guy Lassater knew his stuff, all right. For a minute, he thought about just quitting, just letting that computer nerd win.

The feeling didn't last long. I did it before, I can do it now. I can get through this. I can. I'll just take it step by step. I don't have to hurry. Nobody's timing me.

Chapter Nine

In the week since Jack and Gracie and company had finished refurbishing the storefront, he'd let his concern over his mother and Mike Petrov and their relationship simmer. At least a hundred times, he'd told himself not to pry into his mother's personal business. She and Mike were probably just becoming friends—and that was good, right?

Now, on a bright, unusually warm morning for late June, he drove to his mom's house and jumped out of the car, ready to find out. What was going on? He didn't want his mom hurt, but with her progressive disability, how could she avoid it? What man would want her in a wheelchair? It wasn't right, but that's how the world thought.

"Hi, Jack!" Mr. Pulaski, sporting his favorite straw gardening hat, greeted him over the fence.

Jack paused, realizing how grateful he was that Mr. Pulaski was his mom's neighbor. Jack could always count on the retired cop to keep an eye on his mom. "Hi, how're you?"

"Great." Mr. Pulaski motioned toward Jack's mother's backyard. "Your mom's carpenter is doing great work. They've already got the slab poured and he's getting the frame up."

Jack followed the neighbor's gesture and saw that his mother's addition was indeed taking shape. A cement foundation and wooden frame now connected the house and garage. But the progress aggravated rather than pleased him. Why had she hired someone who might end up hurting her?

"I like that guy," Mr. Pulaski went on. "He's a good worker and your mom's smiling and laughing all the time when he's here."

Not the least reassured, Jack felt his jaw tighten.

"It's about time your mother found someone who appreciates her. Your father didn't know what he had till he left. But that's ancient history. It's just that I'm happy for Sandy. And she says that Mike's been alone for a lotta years, too."

Jack held his tongue, but it was a challenge. He didn't want to think badly of Mike, but based on Jack's experience, his mother could only be hurt when the job ended and Mike left the scene. Jack merely nodded.

"See you, Mr. Pulaski."

Mr. Pulaski turned back to weeding his flower bed.

Jack strode inside the back door. "Mom! It's me, Jack."

His mom, dressed in faded jeans and a rumpled T-shirt, entered the kitchen with only a slight halt in her gait. "Jack, how nice. I didn't expect to see you today."

Why was she dressed in her yard-work clothes? He shrugged. "Just stopped by to say hi and then I'm off to the office."

She hugged him tight once and then turned to the counter. "You've been busy and so have I. Did you see how far we've gotten out back?"

He nodded and sat down at the table.

His mother silently offered him a cup of morning coffee, and he tried to come up with a way to broach the subject: *Uh, Mom, what is it with you and Mike Petrov?* No. *Mom, you seem to be spending a lot of time with Mike Petrov...*

Instead, he blurted out, "Did you know Dad's engaged again?" He cringed inside. That was the last thing he'd wanted to say!

"Yes," his mom replied, pouring two cups of coffee, "I've met her."

"You've met her!" Jack stared at his mother. "Why?"

"Cliff told me about her and they dropped by...oh, several months ago, on their way to some fund-raiser or something. She seemed very nice."

"What is she, a blonde with plenty of cleavage?" Jack couldn't hold back the sarcasm.

"Jack!" Sandy scolded. "I don't like your tone."

He did a slow burn. Why did his mother always take his dad's side? He dourly sipped his hot coffee.

Sandy sat down across from him. She touched his hand. "Jack, what your father did when he left me for someone else was wrong. He made a mistake and he paid for it. Let it go."

You mean you *paid for it!* But Jack made no reply.

"And for your information—" Sandy pulled her hand away and sat back in her chair "—Gloria is a widow about my age and has one grandchild."

Jack's mouth dropped open. "You're kidding."

Sandy shook her head.

"He wants me to meet her."

"You should."

Jack didn't like the grumpy feeling that was taking him over, but he didn't seem to be able to control it. *So go ahead and ask!*

"What's with you and Mike?"

His mother paused in the act of lifting her mug to her lips. She stared at him.

His grumpiness increased and he felt his neck warm around his collar.

"Mike," his mom said in a slow, even tone, "is a very good friend. I enjoy his company and find him attractive. And the rest is none of your business. I never ask about whom you are seeing—"

"*Are* you seeing him?" Jack knew he shouldn't ask this, but he couldn't keep his mouth shut. He'd done that for weeks already.

"But," his mom continued as though she hadn't heard his question, "I think *I* should ask, when are you going to start looking for a wife?"

"A wife?" *What?*

"Yes, when are you going to break out of your preoccupation with computer viruses and look around for a wife? Am I going to have to wait until I'm in my sixties before I become a grandmother?" She challenged him over the rim of her cup.

Why were women always trying to match everyone up? He wasn't a match—period. Then he remembered kissing Gracie and realized that he'd been wanting to repeat that very interesting experiment. His neck became warmer.

He took a bracing sip of coffee. "I don't think about marriage." He'd never said these words, but hadn't he always felt that way? Uncertainty coiled its way through his midsection. "I don't think I'd be a good husband, or father, for that matter."

"You're great with the twins! You'd be an excellent father—"

The back door opened. "Hi, Sandy, it's me. Ready to start work?" Mike, also in work clothes, walked into the kitchen.

Jack glared at his mother.

In return, Sandy smiled at him and whispered, "I love you, but *mind your own business.*"

On Wednesday morning, Gracie looked up from behind her desk as Jack walked—make that *stalked*—

into their freshly redecorated storefront. What was up with Jack?

She didn't know, but she did know now that she would have to build up to her announcement, prepare him. She followed him to his desk at the rear. *I just know he's forgotten. Maybe I shouldn't go. If things weren't so different, so up in the air this year...*

Jack parked himself at his computer and tapped its keys hard enough to break the keyboard.

From a few feet in front of him, Gracie stared at his bent head. The summer sun had begun highlighting the auburn in his hair. He needed a haircut and the hair at his nape was curling up, enticing her to smooth it down. She folded her hands together instead.

"What's up?"

"Nothing." He didn't even glance her way.

"Did the hacker break in again?"

Now he looked up, his handsome faced twisted into a disgruntled frown. "No. Why would you ask that?"

She walked forward and sat down in the chair by his desk—entering dangerous territory, dangerous since she might let her too-keen fascination with this maddening man show. "Well, something's got your socks in a wad—what?"

Moving his jaw as if chewing angry words, very tough gristly ones, he stared at her. "Nothing." He forced out this single word at last. "Where's Patience?'' He motioned toward the desk nearest the front door. ''Why isn't she at her desk?''

Gracie glanced around, proud again of what they'd done with the place. Two coats of white on the walls and the same of finish on the floor, and the place gleamed. ''She's at an Illinois teacher's job fair downtown.''

Undeterred by this ploy, Gracie eyed him. If the man spent half as much time trying to communicate with other humans as he did trying to avoid it... ''Did something happen?''

''Your father—'' he began.

The quaint little bell on the door, left over from the hardware store, jingled. Gracie glanced around and saw Troy's grandmother, whom the twins called Staramama, barreling in. Gracie rose, uncertain moths fluttering in her stomach.

''Good morning. What brings you here today?''

Very plump, with white hair like spun sugar and dressed in a vintage 1957 Sears cotton housedress, Staramama drew herself up to her full height, five feet and no inches. She shook a gnarled finger with several rings on it in Gracie's face. ''You gotta talk to that sister of yours! She's making Troy unhappy! And what about those twins, those sweet little boys?''

Gracie tried not to take offense. ''I'm sure Annie and Troy will work things—''

''My grandson Troy works hard every day to provide a nice home for Annie and the boys. Did she ever have to work one day outside her own house? No, she did not! What's wrong with her?''

Gracie held back a retort. After all, Staramama was nearly ninety years old. She didn't understand—

''Now, you tell your sister that she better get home and tend to business—*her* business—or she'll find herself in the middle of a *mess* she don't count on. She made promises in a church to my grandson and she shouldn't break them!''

''Annie's not breaking her vows.'' Gracie held on to her temper. ''She and Troy can work this out if everyone would just let them—''

''That sister of yours should be happy with her life. What does she need a degree for? My Troy don't need one.''

Gracie gritted her teeth. ''If Troy didn't want Annie, the girl…the woman she is, he should have married someone else. Annie won scholarships and was the valedictorian of her class—''

''That's all in the past!''

''Annie has a wonderful mind and she deserves to follow her dream and go to college!'' Gracie insisted.

Suddenly, Jack was beside her. ''I don't want to be rude, but maybe your grandson better decide on whether he wants Annie and his family back or not. He was acting like a jerk the other night. Why don't you tell him to grow up?''

Pink with anger, Staramama responded sharply with something in Slovenian, her native tongue, and left, banging the door behind her.

Silence.

"Don't let it upset you, Gracie." Jack touched her shoulder.

She couldn't help herself, her hand covered his. And his sympathetic voice nearly caused her to let tears of frustration flow, but she forced them down. She stood so close to him, so near yet still unattainable. The kiss they'd shared flitted through her mind again. *I have to get away! But I can't break away. Why do things keep drawing us together, closer and closer?*

No answers came to her. Every occurrence in the past few weeks had conspired to push them together in spite of her plans.

And now, they'd been interrupted by Staramama's visit. Gracie drew in a deep, fortifying breath. She might as well broach the subject on her mind and get it over with. "I hate to bring this up, but my vacation starts Friday."

"Your vacation?" He stared at her; his hand slid from her shoulder.

She turned to face him. *Jack, I don't want to leave you. But I have to. At least I'll have a week away. Maybe something will intervene...*

"Yes—" she tried to soften the blow "—but I'm not going to take a full two weeks like I usually do."

"Two weeks?" He sounded like her vacation and its length were totally new concepts.

Jack, you'll drive me insane! Then, why did she want to lean closer and press her cheek against his and have him hold her? "Just one week. You know I go north to a cabin my family rents in Wisconsin every June."

"You do?" Jack sounded clueless. He studied her and then added, "That's right. You do."

She couldn't help sighing. She'd been right. Leave it to Jack to completely forget her annual vacation. And she couldn't even blame it on all the uproar and changes they'd faced. Her need for a vacation from work and the idea that she took one yearly had always baffled him.

But unfortunately, this year's wasn't the usual fun family time she always looked forward to, either. "Troy and Annie have refused to go this year," she explained, her chin dipping low. "But my dad persuaded them that the twins shouldn't do without their vacation just because their parents are at loggerheads."

"Loggerheads?"

"Fighting," Gracie explained, very aware of how close Jack stayed.

"Oh."

Jack didn't move or say another word. They stood just inches from one another. She sensed Jack hesitate. Then he moved closer to her and took her arms in his hands.

"Gracie, I stopped to see my mom today and—"

His phone rang. With a sound of disgust, he snatched it out of his pocket. "Jack here," he snarled.

"Jack," his mother said, "I just wanted to let you know that I'm going to be off on vacation next week."

"You are?" Was the whole state of Illinois leaving on vacation? "Where are you going, Mom?"

"To a cabin on a lake in Wisconsin—"

"Gracie just told me—" he was not liking the suspicion that had just come to him "—that she would be gone next week at a place there." *I'm wrong, right? I always get what's going on with people wrong. Why should I be right this time?*

"Well." His mother drew in breath. "As a matter of fact, I'm accompanying Gracie and her dad. I'm going along to help out with the twins. I can't run after them, but I can help with the cooking—"

"What?" He glared at Gracie. He didn't want to be right.

"Now, Jack, don't be…don't be negative. I'm really looking forward to it." His mom sounded cautious.

But he doubted he could get her to change her mind. "If you're going, I'm going, too," he blurted out, resolve hardening in him.

"Jack, don't be silly," his mom objected. "If you and Gracie are away at the same time, who will take care of LIT?"

"The Hope job is done. I have a few smaller projects on board now, but I can still work via modem, while Gracie's cousin and friend take care of the phones. If Troy and Annie are staying home, then you and I can take their places.'' He hung up.

Gracie studied him as though measuring him.

Jack shoved his hands into his pockets. ''I'm going on vacation, too.''

''You are?'' Gracie said, looking nonplussed. ''Where?''

''To that blasted cabin your father rents on a lake in Wisconsin.''

''You can't go.'' Gracie closed the gap between them as if physically prepared to stop him.

''Why not?''

''You just can't!'' she wailed.

''Well, I can and I will. My mom is not going along with your dad without me—''

''My dad…your mom.'' Gracie took a step backward. ''What's going on in that brain of yours? Dad said it would do your mom good to get out of the city. They're just friends.''

''Friends? I don't think so. She says she finds him attractive. That's not something a woman says about a friend.''

''Well, that's their business.'' Gracie looked flushed. ''Not ours.''

''I don't want my mother hurt again.'' Jack bent his head forward and glared at her.

''My father wouldn't hurt anyone!'' Gracie propped her hands on her hips and leaned forward almost nose to nose with him. ''And they don't need a chaperone. They're just friends. Why shouldn't your mom have a week at the lake? Jack, you're being ridiculous. Don't make a mountain out of a molehill.''

Late Friday, near twilight, Gracie leaned back discontentedly with the map open in her lap in the front seat of Jack's car. Andy sat in the back in his car seat. Somewhere ahead of them in the truck, Mike, with Sandy and Austin, preceded them en route to the cabin in northern Wisconsin. Traffic jammed the four-lane highway. Cars with boats and bikes attached swooshed by. Tents strapped on top of vans and RVs zoomed past.

Gracie tried to release the tension in her neck and upper back muscles. How had she gotten so stressed? *Easy answer—I didn't need Jack on my vacation.*

Every time she tried to distance herself from Jack, something intervened and she found herself more closely enmeshed with him than ever before. What was going on? Why was breaking away so impossible lately? And what if Jack was right and her dad and his mom were interested in one another?

She closed her eyes. *Not that—please, Lord. If Dad and Sandy actually are growing closer, it will make Jack totally unavoidable. I'll have him at work and in the family. Nooooo!*

"Aunt Gracie," Andy whined for the seventh time in the past fifteen minutes. "Are we there yet?"

"Not yet, honey." Gracie took a deep breath. "Jack, there's a rest area coming up. We need to stop before it gets dark. I think it's on our right. Watch for it.''

"Stop?" he protested, not taking his eyes from the road. "We can't stop in this traffic. We don't have time to stop. Your dad must be miles ahead of us."

Gracie groaned silently. This was like something in a script of a comedy about a couple on a family trip. "We're traveling with a child, remember?" Gracie tried to keep her voice light. "I told you we'd have to make frequent pit stops."

"But we stopped two hours ago," Jack said in a mystified tone. "At this rate, it will be midnight before we get there!"

"Well," she explained, giving in to feeling world-weary and just plain cranky, "that's *why* I wanted to get away no later than two so we'd avoid the Friday-night weekend getaway traffic—"

"You know I had to get that software problem fixed. GEC Services is one of our most profitable accounts—"

"Let's not go over this again." She tightened her self-control. "Just—there! There's the sign. One half mile on the right," she read.

"I can't stop—"

"*Please,* Jack!" Gracie cut him off. "Stop at the rest area!"

With a swallowed oath, he flipped on his turn signal and turned into the shady parking area. He coasted into the spot under a maple tree and parked.

"Lighten up, Jack," she murmured. "The drive is

part of the experience. The trip is not an endurance race." *For how many centuries have women been saying that?* She envisioned herself in long dusty skirts tromping beside a covered wagon, and Jack saying, *We have to cover two more miles today—we can't stop now!*

Oblivious to the emotional currents in the car, Andy unlatched his special seat belt harness and climbed into the front. "Let's go pump water, Mr. Lassater!"

"What?" Jack looked dumbfounded.

Andy clambered over him, unlatched Jack's door and jumped outside. "Come on. It's fun!"

"Go on. I have to use the facilities," Gracie said, motioning toward the small brick building on her right. "You go and help Andy pump us some water. Have him wash his hands and face, without getting completely soaked!"

Jack didn't reply. Andy was dragging him by the hand toward the covered open-air shelter where another family was washing their hands under the old-fashioned communal hand pump.

Gracie grinned. "I said lighten up, Jack!"

When she returned, she found that Jack and Andy had shed their shoes and socks and were pumping the water just for the fun of it. Liberally dotted with splash marks on his shirt and slacks, Jack was grinning at Andy, who was jumping up and down and yelping at the cold water. Why couldn't Jack always take life like this?

Unfortunately, it only made him more irresistible.

"Having fun yet?" she asked, a smile curving her mouth.

"Come on, Aunty. The water's really good!" Andy invited.

"Aren't we in a hurry?" she asked in an arch tone, sitting down on a picnic bench under the shelter and slipping off her sandals.

"Lighten up," Jack said, grinning at her. "The drive is part of the experience—or something."

She chuckled, invigorated by his attention. "Not bad, Lassater." She held her feet under the icy water as Jack pumped again. "Cold!" she shrieked.

"Yeah! Isn't it great?" Andy crowed. "I wish we had a pump in our backyard. Could Grampa make us one?" He leaped up and down in the spattering water. "Let me pump. Let me!"

Jack lifted the boy so he could reach the dark-green pump handle. Then Andy, with his full forty pounds of weight on it, dragged the handle down.

She shrilled again as the frigid water spurted over her bare feet and ankles. Shivers ran up her legs and the smile that had conquered Jack's aggravated expression nearly overwhelmed her with delicious sensations she couldn't afford to encourage. *Oh, Jack, what am I going to do with you?*

After midnight, Jack peered at a faded wood sign lit only by his headlights, Groshky's Cabins. They'd arrived. Gracie dozed beside him, her cheek against his arm, while Andy slept in his car seat. The vacation had officially begun. Jack couldn't figure out if he was relieved or not. This summer had been full of unexpected changes and surprises. When would he get back to normal? He stared into the darkness, hearing the croaking of frogs and the hoot of an owl. What next? A bear?

Dear Father, what did I get myself into?

Chapter Ten

"**G**ood morning!"

At the sound of excited young voices, Jack blinked open his eyes.

Austin and Andy stood next to where he lay on the couch, staring into his face. "Good morning!" they repeated even louder.

A moment of disorientation and then Jack pulled himself up to a sitting position.

"We're at the cabin!" Andy announced with a leap of excitement.

"Aunt Sandy is gonna make us pancakes!" Austin performed a similar jig.

"Do you like pancakes?" Andy asked in as serious a tone as if he'd just asked Jack if he were in favor of world peace.

Jack managed to nod. *It's real. I'm here in this cabin.* Then he heard his mother speak to Mike and it all came back to him. He was here to keep his mom from being hurt.

"Hi there." Gracie's soft, feminine voice curled down the back of his neck.

It was happening again. He looked up and Gracie was there at the foot of the couch. She wore a deep-blue tank top and cutoffs with ragged hems. Her wet hair was slicked back, but a few drops of water trickled down her neck and wisps of black hair curled around her hairline. She looked gorgeous.

Gracie, what am I going to do? Why can't I stop noticing you? Why can't we just be the way we were a month ago?

Looking away, he combed his hair with his fingers, feeling that he needed a haircut and, more critically, a shower. A cold one.

"Hi."

"It's your turn for the shower now." Gracie sat down on the arm of the couch, her thigh bumping against his blanketed foot.

Keeping his eyes downcast, he swung his feet to the floor.

"Hurry up. Your mom's in charge of breakfast and…" Gracie paused to sniff audibly. "It smells like bacon—"

"And pancakes!" the boys chorused in high spirits.

Aware of the mouth-watering scents of bacon and butter, he rose and heeded Gracie's motion toward a door off the main room of the rustic cabin. It occurred to him as he picked up his duffel bag and entered the small bathroom that Gracie was often telling him what he should do. *I should resent that.*

But he didn't. Existence was so much easier with Gracie there to point the way. With Gracie, he didn't have to think about all the daily minutiae of life. That was Gracie's job, and it left him free to concentrate on what he really wanted to do. What would he do if he lost Gracie?

Why am I thinking about things like this? Was it because of losing Tom or because of what Tom had said about Jack proposing to Gracie so she wouldn't leave? Gracie would never leave him. Still, insecurity trickled through him. So much had changed in the past month.

Pushing these disturbing thoughts aside, Jack surveyed the cramped bathroom—a rusty-looking toilet, sink and aged shower stall with a sad shower curtain—all with barely room to turn around between them. Okay, he knew he hadn't been headed for the Hilton.

"Hurry up, Jack!" his mother called from the kitchen, her cheerful voice a bit faint through the door.

Why does she have to sound so happy? Jack stripped, and cranked on the shower. Standing under the unenthusiastic sprinkle, he let the water rinse the sleep from his eyes.

Recollections of the camping trips he and his parents had taken when he was no older than the twins fluttered into his mind. Those had ended with his dad's entrance into medical school. He'd been much too busy after that. Jack scrubbed his head, rubbing away the memories.

"Come on, Jack! Pan–cakes!" one of the twins yelled, pounding on the bathroom door.

Jack complied quickly, drying off and donning a wrinkled pair of shorts and a T-shirt. He dropped his duffel back at the end of the couch and walked to the round table at one end of the large central room. Mike sat there with the twins on his right side. Gracie was setting the table with chipped plates, mismatched tableware and bright yellow paper napkins. She smiled and motioned him toward the seat next to Andy. He sank into it, not looking toward Mike.

"Morning, Jack," Mike said. "Sounds like you got stuck in the middle of the weekend traffic last night."

Was that a dig or just conversation? Jack shrugged.

His mother appeared at the table with a large platter of fragrant bacon in hand. Gracie came up behind with an even larger platter topped with a listing stack of griddle cakes.

Beaming, Mike rose and took the platter from

Sandy. Jack didn't miss the smile she gave Mike or the way Mike managed to touch his mom's hand in the transfer.

Jack fumed silently. He would get Mike alone for a talk—soon. Maybe Mike didn't realize that he was leading Jack's mom on. Jack would give him the benefit of the doubt until then—but only till then.

Sandy and Gracie sat down, completing the circle.

"Let's say grace," Mike said. He reached for Sandy's and Austin's hands and bowed his head.

Jack took the hand Andy offered him and accepted Gracie's hand in his other. Her hand felt so small, so dainty in his. How could someone so slight and delicate outside be so strong within?

"Dear Father, bless our time together here at the cabin. Give us safety and sunny days. Bless those who stayed at home—Annie, Troy, Patience and Connie. Now we thank you for this delicious food and the loving hands that prepared it. Amen."

"Amen!" the twins shouted. "Pancakes! Please!"

Jack didn't miss the special smiles that Mike and his mother exchanged. He simmered with irritation. The talk with Mike would be sooner rather than later.

The breakfast passed quickly and then Jack was suddenly aware that he had no plan for the day. In his momentary disorientation, he dived for his black laptop case at the end of the couch as if it were a life preserver.

"We're going to go swimming, Mr. Lassater," Andy informed him. "Wanta come?"

Jack stared at them. "Swimming?"

"Yes, Jack. You know—" his mom teased, "you get into water and wave your hands and kick your legs around to keep from sinking."

He held his laptop case in front of him. "I need to check in and see if any of my clients need me. Where's the phone?" He looked around for it.

"Jack, you're on vacation—" Sandy started.

"Don't waste your breath," Gracie said. "Jack, we don't have a phone."

"What? No phone?" He couldn't believe it. "What place doesn't have a phone?"

"Groshky's Cabins are without phones," Mike replied. "People come here to get *away* from phones."

Jack bristled. "People depend on me—"

"Come on, Jack, we'll wean you off your addiction slowly." Gracie sounded amused with him. "There's a phone at the main office. They'll probably let you plug your modem into their phone jack long enough to download your e-mail."

"But," he began, "what if—"

"You're on vacation. I'll help you get your e-mail, but that's it." Gracie beckoned him to come with her. "We left work behind us."

After a short walk among pine trees, Jack trailed Gracie through an aged and scarred wooden screen door into a dilapidated log house near the resort entrance. He recognized it from the night before. Gracie greeted a large woman in her sixties with three chins and flyaway gray hair.

"Hello, Mrs. Groshky." He shook hands with her over a cluttered counter that displayed fishing lures.

Gracie explained what Jack needed.

Mrs. Groshky frowned. "I don't know. We never had no computers here."

"You haven't?" The idea boggled his mind. *No computers?*

"He just needs it to download his e-mail and then he'll plug your phone back in," Gracie explained.

"It won't hurt the phone, will it?" Mrs. Groshky looked leery. "We only got the one line, you know. I like to keep that working in case we had an emergency or somethin'."

Hurt the phone? What planet am I on? Jack tried to keep a straight face.

"It won't hurt the line," Gracie assured her. "And it will only take a few minutes."

"Okay, come behind the counter, then." Mrs. Groshky grumbled and moved her bulky form away from the wall-mounted phone.

Within seconds, Jack had his laptop plugged into the wall jack and was accessing the connection options. "You don't have a local calling number for this area." He looked to Mrs. Groshky. "I'll have to pay you for the call, then. It will be a long-distance charge."

Mrs. Groshky frowned and shook her triple chins in disapproval.

"Jack, you have to give in and admit that we are in the north woods, away from civilization as we know it." Looking amused, Gracie leaned toward him and rested her folded hands on the counter.

Trying not to look at the attractive picture she presented, Jack tapped the keys and listened to the buzzing and tones as the modem dialed the access number.

"Gee, it makes funny sounds. You're sure it don't hurt the phone?" The proprietress watched him as though he were a snake charmer. "I've heard about this e-mail stuff, but I never seen anyone do it before."

"It's not much to watch." Gracie turned her head toward the woman.

"It didn't go through," Jack complained.

"Try again." Gracie leaned farther forward till her head nearly touched Jack's. "What's wrong?"

He shook his head.

"Hey! Mrs. Groshky," a kid yelled as he banged inside, "my dad needs bait."

The woman went over to an old-model refrigerator. "What's he want—night crawlers or red oak worms?"

Ignoring her, the kid stared at Jack.

Night crawlers? Jack hunkered down over his laptop and waited for his ISP to finally make the connection with the outside world.

Another customer, a harassed-looking man in a hat with fishing lures around the brim, arrived to get keys to the cabin they were renting for the week, and stared at him, too. Then a family came in wanting to buy a fishing license and stood gawking at him. Mrs. Groshky squeezed her abundant form around Jack twice and glared at him.

"You almost done?"

Jack felt the urge to toss the laptop out the window. Did everyone think he was on exhibit? Finally, his server made the connection and he watched the transmission percentage progress at a snail's pace until it finally achieved one hundred percent. Success! He scanned the sender's column at the left of his screen.

"Hey, neat computer!" A teen with a buzz cut and a gold earring leaned against the counter. "Does it have any games on it? My dad wouldn't even let me bring my PDA along. Groshky needs to put in some video games."

"Shoo!" Mrs. Groshky waved the teen out. "This is not a toy and this isn't a place where you sit with your head in a computer game when the sun is shining outside."

The teen slunk out, slamming the door behind him.

"I don't know if I want computers here." Mrs. Groshky confronted him, her hands propped on her bountiful hips. "This is a place for putting away computers. Don't you know what a vacation is?"

"I agree. Don't worry, Mrs. Groshky." Gracie hurried him outside. "We'll try not to come during the daytime when you're so busy."

Jack thanked the older woman through the screen door and followed Gracie. "I'll probably check back later—"

"No! You go swimming, fishing, have fun," Mrs. Groshky called after them. "No more computers. This ain't a computer place."

Trying to ignore Mrs. Groshky, Jack watched Gracie walking beside him. He again wondered at the change in Gracie. They'd worked side by side for five years. Why hadn't he noticed the fluid way she walked, the way her perfect nose turned upward at its end?

Gracie strolled beside him, evidently unaware of the effect she was having on him.

"Did you hear anything from any of our clients?"

"Just my dad saying he's glad my project's done and everything's back to normal." Jack silently hoped his dad was right.

"I also think," Jack continued, "I've got enough information to clear that nurse they suspected. But I still wish I could get a lead on who the hacker was."

"Maybe you scared whoever it was out of the hacking business."

"Let's hope so."

On the walk back to the cabin, Gracie racked her brain to come up with a strategy for getting Jack to actually *take* a vacation.

He strode beside her on the dirt path as if they were still on the streets of Chicago. If she didn't stop him now, the vacation could be ruined for everyone. Mrs. Groshky's expression had boded ill for any future attempts to connect to the Internet.

Within sight of their cabin, Gracie decided she had to take action. She slowed. "Jack, we need to talk."

"About what?"

"About whether you should stay or go." Gracie halted and faced him.

"Go? Why?"

She gripped his arm and dragged him into the cover of a tall pine. The chirping birds in the tree flew out, flapping and scattering overhead. "Jack, one of the reasons my family comes here every year is that Groshky's hasn't changed since 1957 when they opened." She released his arm and edged back. How could he look so good in wrinkled shorts and a rumpled T-shirt? "It isn't a computer kind of place—"

"What does that mean?"

Oh, Jack. "It means this is a place you come to forget about work." She pointed to the laptop under his arm. Crows overhead squawked on a lone phone line as though making rude comments at them. "I should not have let you bring that thing here."

"You sound like it's covered with a fatal bacteria." Jack eyed her and shifted restlessly.

"As a matter of fact, it is infected…with anti-vacation bacteria. I'm afraid we are going to have to put it into quarantine."

Jack's proximity ignited tension in Gracie. She tried to ignore how all her nerve endings felt like they had been hooked up to an electric fence.

"And that means?"

Jack sounded baffled and uneasy at the same time. Not a good combination. Undaunted, she inched forward and lifted her chin until their noses were nearly touching. *Why can't I just step back and protect myself?* "That means we're going to put it back in its case and leave it in the closet—"

"Gracie! I've got to check my accounts every day."

She pressed both hands against him, forcing him back farther into the boughs of the pine. Sensations—Jack's solid chest and the evergreen needles and scent—shook her concentration, but she went on. "Going on vacation means not working. That means not checking on accounts, period."

"What if something happens…what if there's an emergency? People, companies depend on me." Jack squawked like the crows.

"I told Patience and Connie to call us here if there is an emergency. They will check the e-mail for us—"

"No, I…" He clutched his laptop to him as if it were a babe in arms.

She laid a hand on the warm skin just below his short sleeve. "You know I'm right." She knew she should break their contact, but couldn't. "I blame myself. I should have prepared you for this, insisted you take a vacation every year for the past five. Then this wouldn't be such a shock to your system."

She leaned closer, irresistibly drawn to him. "Now we're going into the cabin," she informed him gently, "and you're going to put away your laptop."

He shook his head as if in disbelief. "Not my computer."

"Give it to me…please." She held out her hand. "Come on. You know I'm right."

Jack held firm. "Gracie, I… Gracie…"

She closed the final, thin space between them. Why couldn't she keep her distance? His breath fanned the hair over her right ear, making it tickle. She shivered.

"Jack," she said in a soothing voice, "you know I'm right. You want to have fun. You wouldn't have come with us if you hadn't wanted to. You never do what you don't *want* to do. You want to have fun, I know you do."

Jack appeared to be having trouble catching his breath.

"Jack?"

His mouth hovered over hers.

"Jack," she whispered, heat rolling through her body, warming her face.

She heard the twins burst out of the cabin door, pound down the wooden steps and come running. *No, don't interrupt us now!*

"Mr. Lassater, come on! We waited for you to go swimming with us. Come *on!*"

Jack gazed down at her.

What flickered in his eyes? Disappointment? Was he feeling what she was? Seeing the twins from the corner of her eye, she reached for the laptop, but didn't wrest it from his grasp. Then she realized the twins had done her a favor. *That's right! I'll let the twins do the work of persuading him.*

"Jack, we can't go swimming with the laptop," she teased.

"All right." Slowly, he relinquished the laptop to her.

She let out a gasp. "Great. Now we're officially on vacation." She stumbled backward from him— shocked suddenly by her insistence and her success.

And most of all, by how close she'd come to kissing Jack, her boss—again!

She was lucky to have two small boys along. If they couldn't run the best interference between her and Jack, who could?

"Okay, boys, give me and Mr. Lassater a minute to get changed and we'll be right with you."

* * *

The next bright and beautiful morning, all of them sat in the large picnic shelter near the main office. Dressed in shorts and summer dresses, many of the resort guests had gathered for an informal Sunday worship service.

After a full day and night at the resort, Gracie had begun to relax—except when Jack was right beside her, as he was now.

And another cause of tension—in front of them, Mike and Sandy sat shoulder to shoulder. That didn't bother her much. But watching Jack stare at the backs of their two parents did. Jack might be right for once. Sandy and Mike might be more than friends.

Then, before Gracie's startled eyes, her dad put his arm around Sandy's shoulders. So Jack had been right. Her dad and his mom were…an item.

Conflicting emotions cascading through her, she glanced up at Jack. The stormy look on his face told her that he hadn't failed to notice her dad's move. She felt blindsided herself.

A hymn was announced and they all rose, holding a tattered sheet with words to several traditional songs. Someone strummed a guitar and began, *"What a friend we have in Jesus."*

Jack shifted on the seat and probably not because the bench was hard.

"All our sins and griefs to bear," Gracie joined in, observing how her dad and Sandy shared a song

sheet. Well, she couldn't have chosen anyone better for her dad. The only problem now—Jack. She leaned close to his ear. "Don't be so obvious," she whispered.

He glanced at her, obviously disgruntled.

"Let it go."

Now he glared at her.

Dear Lord, what am I going to do with this man? He's going to upset his mom if he keeps this up. And she doesn't deserve that.

"What a privilege to carry everything to God in prayer," Gracie sang in her tenuous soprano voice. *This is hard, Lord. I didn't think my dad would marry again. But he has a right to love again. I know that.* Still, she felt a stitch in her side, a growing pain.

Her mother's face floated through her mind. Her mother had been gone nearly a decade. And Sandy was definitely a sweetheart. Gracie swallowed down her own emotional reaction to her father becoming interested in another woman. *"Oh, what peace we often forfeit,"* she sang. *"Oh, what needless pain we bear. All because we do not carry everything to God in prayer."*

The hymn ended and everyone shuffled around and reseated themselves.

Andy promptly climbed onto Jack's lap while Austin hurried around the bench and clambered onto his grampa's lap. Austin put his arms around Mike's neck and stared over Mike's shoulder at Gracie and Jack.

"I'm not a preaching pastor," said a slight man in his early thirties who was standing at the front. The wind blew his long hair around and he pushed it away from his face. "I'm a youth pastor at a church in Milwaukee. But the Groshkys asked me to give a brief message today in this beautiful natural setting."

His easy conversational style made his congregation settle down and give him their attention.

"As I stand here, I'm filled with gratitude for the opportunity to be able to steal away from the city for a week of sunshine, swimming and fishing."

The audience responded with applause and some murmurs of agreement. "God has created a beautiful world. But man, because of his desire for his own way, has caused a lot of problems. Here it's almost easy to forget that drugs are destroying lives and evil men plot murder. But we're taking a vacation from all that."

Gracie and the people around her sobered. She thought of the hacker and whether he would try to breach Jack's new system.

"Use this time away from everyday responsibilities," the preacher continued, "to tell each other the things you've been too busy to say, like 'I love you.' 'You mean everything to me.' 'I'll do whatever it takes to fix things between us.' 'You're right.'"

A few chuckled at the last phrase.

The youth pastor grinned. "I say that final one a lot. Maybe I need to say it even more often." He glanced at a pretty young mother in the front row and grinned. "I don't think I have to belabor the point."

"I'd just like to remind you that the Lord wants us to settle any disagreements or grudges we have before we come to him to worship. In his Sermon on the Mount, Christ said..." He lifted his Bible and read, "'You have heard that the law of Moses says, do not murder. If you commit murder, you are subject to judgment. But I say, if you are angry with someone, you are subject to judgment....'"

Gracie glanced at Jack. *You are angry, Jack. Please let it go.*

"Jesus goes on to teach the crowd who had gathered in a natural setting, just as we have gathered here, The Lord's Prayer. Let's stand and recite it together." The preacher raised his hand.

The informal congregation rose. Jack held a drowsy Andy in his arms while Mike held Austin.

"Our Father who art in Heaven." The pastor led them.

When they came to the part "Forgive us our trespasses as we forgive those who trespass against us," Gracie glanced up at Jack's sober face. *If only you could read my mind, my heart and accept my love.*

* * *

The next day, Gracie and Sandy were in the kitchen making dinner. At the table, Sandy sat stirring a deep chocolatey brownie mix from a box. At the sink, Gracie rinsed and began tearing lettuce for a salad. In the large room behind the women, the boys were taking a break on the couch and watching the only cartoon show on the only station they could get on the cabin's ancient rabbit-eared TV. Outside the kitchen window over the sink, Jack and Mike were grilling chicken.

Gracie listened to the cartoon antics and Sandy stirred the batter in the bowl while humming to herself. Jack and Mike stood on opposite sides of the grill with their hands in their pockets—the picture of men avoiding one another.

Gracie sighed.

"Are they still acting like jerks?" Sandy asked.

Surprised, Gracie turned, but grinned. "I'm afraid so."

"What are we going to do with them?" Sandy broke another egg into the batter.

Gracie looked out the window. Her dad glanced at Jack and said something. "Dad just said something to Jack," she reported.

"Good." Sandy cracked another egg.

Gracie studied Jack, waiting for him to respond. Finally, Jack said something. Her dad nodded. "Jack finally said something."

"Wow," Sandy crooned. "They better be careful—they might actually start a conversation. What's wrong with men?''

Gracie shrugged. ''Hold it! They're facing each other.''

''Wow!''

''And now…Dad's talking and Jack's listening.''

''Be still my heart!'' Sandy pressed a hand to her chest.

Gracie chuckled. It was a relief to laugh about the tension between the two men in their group. She, and evidently Sandy, too, had been aware of it though they hadn't discussed it.

But more reassuring was the way Jack's stiff posture was loosening and the way he was actually listening to her dad.

I don't know what they're talking about, but thank You, Lord.

Five days later, after night had cloaked the sky above the tall pines, Jack and Gracie stood in front of the cabin. Though it was well after their bedtimes, Austin and Andy stood between them. The four of them all stared above at the full moon. Though happy to have the boys with them, Gracie thought fleetingly of basking in the moonlight with only Jack.

''Okay now, boys—'' Jack looked down into their upturned faces ''—I'm going to show you how to find the North Star, just like my dad showed me when we were on a camping trip.''

This comment surprised Gracie. Jack rarely mentioned his father and especially not in terms of happy memories.

"What's the North Star?" Austin asked, his chin pointing skyward.

"That's the star that people use to find their way at night if they get lost," Jack said.

"Uh-huh," Andy agreed. "But we're not lost."

"Well, you need to know this before you ever get lost," Jack explained.

The twins nodded at this bit of wisdom.

Gracie smiled because she knew that Jack's star lesson was way beyond the boys, but the attention he was giving them could only be good. And in two days, they'd be back in Chicago.

Dear Lord, please let Annie and Troy make progress before we get home. I don't want them to break up. They do love each other!

"Now…" Jack dropped to his knees on the pine needle-littered ground in front of the cabin, so he was at the boys' level. "Look up there. Follow my arm." He raised his arm toward the night sky.

Andy leaned against Jack's right shoulder while Austin leaned against the left. Both boys stared upward.

"Now I'm pointing to the Big Dipper—"

"What's a dipper?" Austin asked.

"It's a…it's a—" Jack fumbled for a word.

"It's like a cup with a long handle," Gracie supplied. It was easy to see why the twins adored Jack. He gave them his full attention. How did he know how to do that?

"Right." Jack grinned at her.

"And that's the big one?" Andy asked.

"Yes," Jack said. "Watch how I trace it. It's just like your connect-the-dots books. See, here's the bowl of the cup and here's the long handle—"

"Is it a bowl or a cup?" Andy asked, leaning harder against Jack.

"The bowl is the round deep part of a cup that holds liquid," Gracie said, as the lake breeze wafted around her ankles.

I wish there weren't so many cross-currents here. I need to know more, understand better. Why had Jack turned against his dad when Sandy and Cliff broke up? Why had he taken it as a personal betrayal, when others in the same situation didn't?

"Oh," Austin said.

"And now the North Star is over in this direction…" Jack continued.

The boys imitated Jack as he rotated to the right.

"Here's the Little Dipper, and the North Star is directly at the top of the handle." Jack put an arm around each boy. "How's that?"

"Ooh…" the twins enthused.

Had Cliff been like this when Jack was a child? He must have been, or how could Jack know just how to behave with the twins?

Mike and Sandy came down the porch steps behind them. "Can you two put the twins to bed?" Mike asked. "We're going to go for a moonlight stroll."

"Sure," Gracie replied.

"Have fun," Jack said. "We'll get the twins turned in."

Gracie looked up at Jack's expression. His words had come out easily and without any edge. Had he accepted the fact of their parents as a couple?

After telling the twins to mind, Mike and Sandy wished them good-night and strolled away, holding hands.

Soon, Gracie and Jack settled the twins into their bunk beds and, without exchanging a word, wandered back out onto the porch again.

"What a beautiful night," she murmured, looking out at the moonlight rippling like silver lace on the water.

Jack came up behind her. "Do you think my mom will be okay with your dad? I mean…not just tonight, but…as a couple? Will they be all right together?"

Chapter Eleven

Gracie turned to look at him. The intense expression on his face drew her closer. How could she make him understand? No matter—she had to try. Her peace of mind and that of everyone else concerned depended on it.

"Of course, Jack. They're already great together. Don't you see that?"

Chin down, he nodded.

"Then, that's good, right?" she ventured, edging closer to him.

Turning away, he gazed out at the lake. "I just never thought Mom would get serious with anyone again."

"Why not?" This was more than mere possessiveness on Jack's part. She could feel it.

Leaning away from her, he propped his hands on

the rough porch railing. ''Because of her health problems…how bad she felt after my dad left her and *before* he left her.''

After his reply, Gracie's hope of persuading him to accept her dad and his mom together faltered. To describe his attitude as glum fell short. To progress up to merely glum, he'd have had to sound much more cheerful.

''Jack—'' she touched his arm tentatively ''—your mom is a wonderful woman. But when I realized that you were right, that my dad was interested in your mom as more than a friend, it surprised me, too.''

''Why?'' He settled onto the porch railing with one knee bent. He faced her. An owl hooted in the distance.

''He loved my mother so.'' Gracie felt her throat thicken. ''Mom's been gone almost ten years and he's never dated anyone.''

''Never?''

His white shirt glowed in the moonlight, making it her focus. Her fingers itched to stroke its soft cotton. She shook her head. ''When she'd been gone about a year, friends started trying to 'fix' him up with dates. But he wouldn't have anything to do with it. Mom was too special.''

''What happened to your mother?'' Jack leaned forward.

His nearness made her quiver. ''Cancer. She got sick the year before I started high school and they thought they caught it, but it came back after a year and then…'' Gracie lifted her shoulders a fraction of an inch. Speaking of her mother's death still had the power to cast a pall over her. "She just got worse and worse." She paused. "It was hard to lose her."

He rose in one smooth motion. His strong arms went around her. "I'm sorry."

She inhaled sharply. How long had she yearned to be right where she was—in Jack's arms? *I shouldn't allow this. I should pull away. I'm not like my mom, not like Annie. I'm not that special. No one could love me the way they were loved. But Jack needs me…maybe…* Stopping her thoughts, she relaxed against him, luxuriating in his solid strength. *I need you, Jack. I don't want to but I do.*

"I was a senior in high school when my dad left," Jack murmured into her hair.

Gracie held her breath. Jack rarely ventured into personal emotional territory. Aside from knowing about his antagonism toward his dad, all she knew of his past, Sandy had told her as a friend.

"I'd gotten used to Dad being gone all the time. His schedule was crazy. But it always had been. But one morning, I came down to breakfast and Mom was crying…" His arms tightened around her.

She pressed closer to him. *Oh, Jack, I hear how much this wounded you.*

"I'd never seen my mom cry before." He paused to suck in air. "It shook me up. She wouldn't tell me what was wrong. But then I started watching her and I noticed how Dad had been coming home later and later and how a lot of nights he was away. I'd always thought he was at the hospital with an emergency operation, so I hadn't questioned it.''

"He was cheating?'' Gracie rested her cheek on the vee of skin at his open collar. His flesh was warm and reassuring in spite of this emotional storm.

"Well, he got married a week after the divorce was final.'' Jack's tone dripped with sarcasm. "I think that's a telling indicator that he had been having an affair while he was still married.''

"Oh, Jack, how awful for Sandy, for you.'' Sliding her cheek to his shoulder, she gazed up into his face.

"It was worse for my mother. I couldn't forgive my dad for making her cry. And he'd really used her.''

"Used her? How?'' Her hands resting on his shirt, Gracie pulled back to get a better view of his expression. Sandy had never mentioned this.

"They married young—in their undergrad years. My mom quit school and began working to support them. Over the years, she managed to get her degree, but she was the primary wage-earner until my dad finished his medical school and residency.''

"I didn't know that.'' Gracie recalled how Jack had immediately taken Annie's side against Troy for reneging on their agreement. This explained Jack's immediate and negative reaction to Troy.

A loon wailed from the other side of the lake as though scolding them.

"It wasn't fair," Jack muttered. "They had a deal. Mom worked to help put him through school and *she* should be benefiting from her hard work today, not some other woman."

Of course Jack would insist on fairness. "This world is often unfair." Gracie smoothed his shirt with her hands, feeling the contours of his chest under her fingertips. "But your mom never seems bitter about Cliff."

"She says I should forgive him. She has." He leaned his stubbly chin onto her forehead.

She slid her arms around him and clasped them behind his back. "I think she's right, Jack. Forgive others as God forgives us. You know that."

"What about justice?" His voice was hard.

She felt the movement of his chin as he spoke. Never had she felt so connected to Jack as she did at this moment. Despite the depressing topic, her heart soared with a silent joy. "That's God's business, not ours."

"That's easy to say, hard to do." He pulled her even closer. "Just look at your sister's situation. Aren't you angry about how Troy and his family are trying to say your sister is not keeping her vows?"

They were so close, she felt each word expand his chest.

Lord, what's happening here? Jack is finally opening doors he's kept shut for years. I've always wanted this closeness, but am I reading too much into it?

She brought her mind back to the topic at hand. "Yes, but their opinions are motivated by their love for Troy. And in the end, they won't matter. I have to keep an open heart or irreparable damage could be done to our family, and Austin and Andy would suffer the most."

"I don't want those little guys hurt. I hate divorce." Jack's voice roughened.

"God doesn't like it either. He knows that it only brings broken hearts. But it happens, and we are responsible for how we behave after one takes place." She closed her eyes and breathed in the clean fragrance of soap mingled with Jack's scent. "Holding grudges does no one any good. Jack, your mom has gone on with her life—"

"I've gone on with mine," Jack insisted gruffly.

"Have you? I know you wouldn't let your dad help you with college costs or start-up capital for LIT. Even now, you didn't want to take a contract with his hospital." She opened her eyes. "What else have you been cutting yourself off from just because you don't want anything from your dad?"

"I just don't want him to think I need him." Jack wouldn't meet her eyes.

"He's family." To emphasize this point, Gracie pulled away a few inches from Jack and made eye contact. "Family helps out family. It's just natural."

"Well, not for me. Sometimes connections are broken and can't be fixed." His voice was harsh.

Gracie let her face rest against Jack's shirt again. She could hear his heart pounding with the intensity of his emotion.

How does a person repair a heart or a family, Lord? Is this what is going to happen to Annie and Troy? Oh, no, please don't let it. Tears sprang to her eyes and she suppressed a sob.

"Are you crying?" Jack smoothed the hair back from her face.

"I'm just worried for Annie and Troy." More tears fell.

"Their situation isn't like my mom and dad's. He's not cheating on her." His uneasy statement sounded more like a question.

Gracie recalled Annie walking and laughing with that young man in the union cafeteria. There would be temptation for Annie on campus, a lot of temptation. She was so pretty, so smart. No, that couldn't be right. Annie would never be unfaithful to Troy. It wasn't in her.

But tears still flowed down her cheeks. She brushed them aside with her fingertips.

"Don't cry, Gracie," Jack whispered, his breath on her face.

She felt him kiss her forehead. Unable to stop herself, she lifted her face to him.

For a long moment, an eternal moment, he merely

looked down into her eyes. And then he lowered his mouth to hers.

Their lips met, tentatively—just a whisper of sensation. Then he cupped the back of her head in one hand and kissed her more deeply.

She tangled her fingers in his soft cotton shirt. His lips played over hers and she was aware of each nuance, each breath they shared. She whispered his name, but heard it only in her heart.

He finally ended the kiss, pulling his lips from hers. She clung to him, uncertain of her footing.

"I'm sorry. I shouldn't—"

She rose on tiptoe and kissed away his apology. Then she whispered, "Don't say you're sorry, Jack. I wanted you to kiss me."

"Why didn't you say so? I've wanted to kiss you again for days—"

This made her laugh. "Jack! I know you think I'm your mind reader, but I'm not."

He didn't reply, only tucked her closer to him. "I've thought about what Tom said about you over and over."

"What did Tom say?" Gracie asked, her words trembling in her throat.

"Don't you remember?" he said evasively.

"Tom said a lot of things," she stalled. *You have to say it, Jack! I can't do this for you!* "Tom is a talker. Which particular words of wisdom?"

"He said I ought to propose to you because what

would I do without you,'' Jack mumbled, sounding uncertain.

Gracie went still, barely breathing. ''Propose?''

''He's right. I would be lost without you. Without you, life doesn't make sense. Does *that* make sense?''

Now that he'd said it, she chuckled, her tension lifting. ''Knowing you as I do, yes, that makes sense.''

He squeezed her tighter. ''Very funny. But would you— Can I...''

''Can I what?'' She lifted an eyebrow.

''Would you consider going out with me? I mean, on a date.''

''What a novel idea.'' Gracie couldn't help but see the humor in the situation, no matter how intense her reaction. She suppressed a smile. Jack's first attempt at love talk had come out in pure Jack style. But would this be wise? Could it work out between Jack and her? *I'm afraid, Lord.* ''You and me on a date? Are you sure? We work so closely together. Maybe—''

''Don't say that. I've been blind to how much I needed you and just how important you are to me. I don't know how to put it into words, and if I try, I'll probably end up saying it all wrong. But what I want to know— Will you give us a chance?''

The sound of paddles swishing through the water broke the silence—someone out in a small boat enjoying the moonlight. Too soon this special time away would end.

Gracie pondered Jack's words. As a declaration of love, it left a lot to be desired. But then, this was Jack and he was right. If he attempted to put his feelings into words, he would probably not do a very eloquent job. And he was also right about needing her—but would that substitute for loving her?

I should say no. But what if… "Okay, Jack, I'll give us a chance."

His mouth claimed hers again. She closed her eyes and kissed him as she had longed to for years. *Is this actually happening? It feels too good to be true.*

"Gracie!" A voice called her from behind. "Mr. Computer! Hey!"

Gracie turned and saw Mrs. Groshky waving a slip of paper. She and Jack pulled apart.

Mrs. Groshky huffed toward them. "Sorry to interrupt." She gave them an appraising look and then winked at Gracie. "But Mr. Computer got a telegram."

"A telegram?" Jack said as he stepped forward to accept the paper.

"Yeah, they called it in to the office just now and I wrote it down just like the Western Union guy read it off. I can't remember anybody getting a telegram here in years!"

"Why would someone telegraph?" Grace asked. "Why not call on the cell phone?"

Jack grimaced. "I turned it off this morning. No-

body had called and our vacation was nearly over."
He handed the paper back to Mrs. Groshky. "You'll
have to read this to me. I can't read your writing."

"Well, I was kind of flustered, you know, and
scrambling around to get something to write on."
Mrs. Groshky lifted her reading glasses, which were
suspended on a chain around her neck, and began,
"Okay, he said— 'New security breached. STOP.
Hope Medicare and Medicaid accounts tampered
with. STOP. Need you back stat. Signed, Cliff Lassater.'"

"Oh no." Gracie's heart sank to her toes.

On Monday morning after his week's vacation, in
the Hope central financial office, Jack scanned the
faces of the Board members as they sat, clustered
around desks. "I've looked at the files and I've found
traces of the hacker, but no solid clues."

The Board members stared back at him. No one
said one word in reply.

"Where do we go from here, Jack?" his father
finally asked.

Jack was aware that he didn't feel the same tug of
resentment toward his dad as he usually did. "But
you need to come up with some more names. I have
to have some new suspects or I can do nothing." He
didn't dare add—with Dr. Collins staring at him—
that he didn't have enough evidence to make any
charges against Collins or Witte. *There has to be
someone else with a grudge against Hope.*

"You mean, this might happen again?" Dunn asked, sitting by a computer behind Cliff.

"It will keep on happening until I can catch the hacker, and I'll be able to do that only when I get some more names from you." Jack wondered why he felt so differently in his dad's presence today. Had it been the vacation? What he'd learned about his mom, Mike, his new feelings toward Gracie? Had that made a difference?

"We're not psychics," Dunn sneered. "What are you going to do if we can't come up with any new names?"

"Then, I'll have to…" Jack fell silent. How could he get them on board once and for all?

"What?" his dad asked. "What will you have to do?"

Jack shook his head. "We're in a public place. I can't know that we're not being overhead or observed or listened to electronically."

"And I'm here," Dr. Collins said with a sarcastic smile.

Board members looked around the room.

"Aren't you exaggerating?" Cliff asked.

"No, and I'm not taking any chances, Dad." Jack surprised himself. He hadn't called his father "Dad" in public for years.

Cliff must have noticed this, too, because he looked up suddenly, his gaze fixed on Jack.

"Where do we go from here?" Dr. Brown leaned

forward in her chair. "What can you do to protect our system while still investigating?"

"I'll have to move your software up to the next level of security." Jack scanned their faces again. Did one of them know something they weren't telling or weren't aware of? "I'll go in and bring your security up to the level that a national defense contractor would have to maintain."

"Will that do it?" Cliff asked, obviously dubious.

Jack shook his head. "It's only a stopgap...until one of you comes up with a suspect who pans out."

His dad had asked a favor of him just before this meeting started. What should he do? Agree or decline? *I'd better ask Gracie. She'll know. She always knows.*

"Why didn't you tell me Dad was interested in your boss's mother?" Annie, in jeans and a navy-blue T-shirt, sat across from Gracie in the Polska Café for late lunch on the Monday after vacation. The café had taken on that relaxed-after-the-rush atmosphere. Mama Kalanovski was in the kitchen with her husband, sharing a late lunch. The two sisters had the place to themselves.

Early this morning, Gracie had called to invite her sister to lunch to find out if things were any better between Annie and Troy. *Lord, I want them back together again, before they hurt Austin and Andy, before they hurt each other too much to forgive.*

Gracie stirred her iced tea again, trying to keep her

restless mind on Annie and Troy and Dad and Sandy, not on her and Jack.

"I didn't know. I mean, I should have guessed but you know…"

"Know what?" Annie pressed her.

"Dad hasn't shown any interest in anyone since Mom passed away. I just figured he wasn't going to look for someone else." Gracie glanced over her shoulder, watching for Jack to walk by the window, returning from his meeting with the Hope Board.

"You remember Mom so much better than I do," Annie said wistfully. "I was only twelve when she died and she'd been sick so long then."

"She was a wonderful woman, a very special person." Gracie's spirits were sinking. Everything that had happened in the past week—Dad and Sandy, Jack and her—had stirred up the past, the sad past.

"I do remember she was always singing…and baking something delicious. And the house was always full of our friends, especially Connie! I wanted to be just like Mom."

"You are like her. I never was." Gracie ran her forefinger around the rim of her iced tea glass. A grilled Reuben sat on the plate untouched. She had no appetite.

Annie eyed her. "I don't know what you mean."

"She was popular like you." Gracie felt the tug of inferiority she always did when she compared herself to her sister and mother. *I try not to be jealous, Lord, but it's hard.* "Dad told me how popular Mom was when she was young and dating. He said everyone wanted to marry her.''

''Well, then, I'm not like her,'' Annie objected, as she lifted her glass. ''Troy was the only one—''

''You know that's not true! You could have dated anyone in high school, but you chose Troy.'' *Don't try to make me feel better, Annie.*

''I don't know about the dating anyone I wanted, but you're right. I chose Troy. What about you and the Brain?'' Annie nibbled her poppy seed roll.

Annie's question shocked her. ''You mean me and Jack?'' Gracie's pulse spiked.

''Yes.'' Annie wiggled a finger at her. ''I notice he's around more and more, and I saw how he pitched right in to help you. And then he goes on vacation with you! I know you've had feelings for him—''

''How did you know that?'' Gracie stared at her smug-looking sister.

''I know you.'' Annie gave her an insouciant grin. ''I saw how you looked when you talked about him. Well, has he finally woken up and noticed you? Has he?''

Gracie sighed. *He's noticed that he needs me. Does he love me? Needing isn't the same as loving.* ''He asked if we could start dating.''

''Wow—good for him. There's hope for all of us, then,'' Annie kidded her with a broad smile.

''Don't tease.'' Gracie blushed warmly. ''What about you and Troy?''

Annie's expression sobered and she put down her roll. "I chose Troy and I still choose Troy."

"What went on between you two while we were all gone?" Gracie tried to keep her voice light.

"When I came over to help him pack the twins for the lake, we declared a truce. And he asked me if I would go with him to the pastor to talk things over." Annie pursed her lips.

"Did you go?"

Annie nodded, staring down.

Grace's tension eased. She took a deep breath. "I'm glad. What caused him to—"

"To behave so responsibly?" Annie asked, the usual repartee back in her tone.

"Annie," Gracie scolded.

"I'm sorry, Sis, but Troy hasn't been acting like himself. He's usually so easygoing. He's been so mad at me."

"You've been angry, too," Gracie pointed out.

Annie nodded. "I know. I've been angry with him ever since Christmas. I finally got the courage to confront him with it."

"With what?" Gracie sat up straighter.

"Gracie!" Connie hurried in and headed right for them. "Come quick. A client is on the phone for you."

Chapter Twelve

Very late that afternoon, Jack stalked into their office next to the Polska, his shoulders hunched.

Gracie had been watching, waiting for him all afternoon. She rose from her desk, trying to control her face that insisted on smiling. *I have news for you, Jack.*

"Hi, how did the Hope meeting go?" she said instead, controlling her voice, keeping it composed.

He lifted his shoulders and then let them drop. "Hard to tell. I told them they have to get busy and get me some leads about who might be doing this."

She studied his disgruntled face. She repressed the urge to hurry to him and put her arms around him. "Had they frozen the corrupted files?" she asked, already guessing the answer.

"Of course not." Jack shoved his hands into his

pockets. "Someone who *thought* they knew how to track the accessing of files decided to take a look—"

"Oh no." She sank back into her chair.

"Yes, a red alert via memo wasn't enough of a deterrent to this *helpful* person," Jack growled. "I still had some untouched files to look through, but they proved inconclusive."

"I'm sorry."

Connie breezed in from the break room in the back. "Greetings. I'm heading out. What do you think of our big news, boss?"

"Big news?" Jack looked at her and then Gracie.

"I didn't have a chance to tell him yet." Gracie shook her head at Connie, having trouble breathing evenly. Would Jack pull her into his arms and—

"Well, tell him!" Connie almost danced with her excitement.

Gracie's stomach fluttered dangerously. She cleared her throat. "Jack, I negotiated my first solo contract. It's not much—"

"Not much!" he scoffed, taking a step closer. "Who?"

Gracie's spirits soared at his instant interest and appreciative expression. "It's a new group of doctors in Oak Park. It's not big like the Hope—"

"Isn't that great?" Connie cut in.

Jack beamed. "Sounds like a good time to celebrate. How about steak at Sharkey's?"

"Oh, Jack…" Gracie tried to keep things in perspective in spite of her mounting elation. "It's not that big—"

"Grab your purse. I'm hungry." He turned to Connie. "Coming with us?"

"No, I've got to get home," Connie said primly, her gaze on Gracie.

"Will you close up shop for us, then?" Jack asked over his shoulder as he led Gracie toward the door.

"Sure!" Connie winked at Gracie.

Gracie felt her face warm, but she allowed Jack to lead her out to the alley where his car was parked.

A new client. *I did it!*

By the candlelight at Sharkey's, Jack gazed across the booth toward Gracie. Whenever he looked at her tonight, he remembered those moments by the lake just two days ago. Two days ago. How had it all come about? Had he really kissed Gracie and asked if they could start a dating relationship? *Do I have feelings for Gracie? Yes, I do!*

The waiter delivered their salads and ground spicy fresh pepper onto their lettuce. Jack gazed at Gracie as she thanked the waiter. Her gray eyes were open wide in the low light of the restaurant and her golden skin glowed with a hint of pink on her cheeks. How long had he merely ignored how lovely Gracie was? *I've been walking around blind. I never thought about love and marriage...*

"I'm very happy with the ways things are turning out," he said, breaking the silence after the waiter's departure. His voice dragged along the bottom of his throat. *Marriage—where had that thought come from? I'm feeling so much, Gracie! But how do I get it out into words? How do I let you know, how do I say it?*

"It's just a small account, Jack—"

"No. I'm not talking about business." He stopped to sort out his emotions, what he wanted to say to her.

He watched her gaze back at him, her fork poised over her salad. Her slim wrist reminded him of how slight, how fragile she had felt in his arms. A contradiction. So delicate, but so strong. So necessary to him.

"It's this, Gracie…I like the fact that we're working together." He folded his hands and stared at them, afraid to look at her. "I like the storefront in your neighborhood. I like it that you are more than my executive assistant." He paused. "I don't know how to say what I'm…feeling."

"I think I understand." Her small, light hand covered his.

He looked up, urging her silently to put his thoughts into words, one of things he most valued in Gracie.

"I think you're trying to say that losing Tom could have ruined everything, but we've handled the changeover well. And now that I've brought us in our first new account, we know that we can go on. LIT isn't going to suffer from losing Tom."

"That's part of it." He reached over and touched her hand. "I'm glad I went on vacation with your family. It was fun and I'm glad I got to know your dad better."

She closed her hand over his.

He wanted to add, *I liked kissing you. I have feelings for you.* But this was too public a place for that kind of declaration. "I'm glad we got to know each other away from the office. I'm glad you're here with me tonight." Revealing this much shook him.

"I'm glad you came to Wisconsin with us, Jack." Her voice had softened. "But I warn you—you're going to take another vacation next year." She aimed her fork at him and then pierced a cherry tomato.

Relieved, he chuckled. "You're scaring me. Mrs. Groshky is one tough cookie."

"Eat your salad." She tapped his hand and then popped the tomato into her mouth.

He obeyed her. But from under his lashes, he watched her eat her salad. How could she be so fascinating? This was just Gracie!

Later, Jack walked Gracie to her back door. The summer evening was still warm, the usual for July in Chicago. As they had strolled up through the backyard, he'd taken her hand. All the doubts he'd had about not knowing how to talk to Gracie had faded. *How could I have known how easy it would be to fall for Gracie?*

But he had something he had put off asking her,

something that would push him to make more changes. *Will this work or is it going to be one big mistake?* He had no doubt what Gracie's reply would be. She would do what was right. He could trust her in that way.

In the faint light from a small fixture beside the back door, she bent over her purse and dug inside for her key ring. When she brought it out, he reached for it.

"Not so fast." He pulled her into his arms and pressed his face into her fragrant hair. "This is pleasure, not business, remember?"

He heard her sigh, a pleasant sound, especially when she relaxed against him, not pulling away. *This is right. It feels so right.*

He bent and claimed her mouth, losing himself in the sensations of her soft lips and then a second sweet sigh. He ended the kiss and held her closer to him.

"I have a favor to ask." Jack breathed in the appealing scent that clung to her hair.

"What?" She looked up.

He cupped her face with his hands. The moment felt poetic. *How delicate. How lovely is my Gracie.* If only he had the courage to say these words.

"What, Jack?" she whispered.

He kissed her mouth once, twice, three times. Closing his eyes, he leaned his forehead against hers. "My dad wants me to have dinner with him tomorrow evening. He wants me to meet his fiancée. Would you come with me?''

''Meet his fiancée?'' She hesitated while he waited for her reply.

Then her arms hugged him tighter. ''Of course. I'd be glad to, *if* you're going to give the woman a chance.'' Her tone turned doubtful.

He'd asked himself the same question. ''I will— or at least I'll try.'' He rolled his forehead back and forth against hers, relishing their closeness. ''Mom says she's a nice grandmotherly-type woman.''

''Well, good.'' Gracie kissed his nose.

Jack claimed her lips again. *Gracie, you make me feel like I can do anything!*

''Hey— Oh, it's you two.'' A voice interrupted the kiss.

Jack and Gracie both turned to see Troy mounting the back steps, but Jack didn't release her.

''Sorry to intrude.'' Troy grinned at them. ''I'm just returning from taking Annie home.''

''You look different,'' Jack observed, ''from the last time I saw you.''

''I feel different. Hey, thanks for pitching in and being so good to my guys at the lake. They told me all about you and fishing and swimming. Oh, and I had to hear about the North Star and dippers.''

''I enjoyed it myself.'' Jack held out one of his hands.

''Great.'' Troy shook hands and then passed around them. ''Sorry I interrupted. Go right on with what you were doing.'' He gave another grin. ''Good night.''

After he'd gone inside, Jack looked down at Gracie. ''What gives?''

''While we were away, he and Annie started going to counseling and working things out. She hopes to move back home by the end of summer.'' Gracie traced the line of his jaw.

Her light touch filled him with longing. ''Really? How did that happen?'' He stole a tiny kiss.

''Annie said the counseling's really helping. Both of them had made assumptions about marriage and being parents without checking to see if their assumptions matched.''

''Do they match now?'' Jack nuzzled the soft skin of her nape.

''I guess that's what they are working on now. Remember when Staramama came in and gave me trouble about Annie?''

''Yes.'' Jack buried his face into the soft hair behind her ear.

''Well, Staramama has been causing trouble all along. She doesn't like it that Annie wants to have an education and she has been interfering.''

''I'm not surprised.'' Jack pressed kisses along her hairline.

''Anyway,'' Gracie went on, trying to concentrate, ''at Christmas Annie overheard her tell Troy that he should just get Annie pregnant again like he did on their honeymoon and that would keep Annie from going back to school.'' Gracie sounded breathless.

He tried to put together what she was saying. ''What?''

''Yes, I know. Anyway, that made Annie suspicious because she always thought that her getting pregnant on their honeymoon just happened.''

Concentrating, Jack paused, his face buried in the cleft between her neck and soft shoulder.

''So this possibility really steamed Annie,'' Gracie continued. ''And when Troy tried to persuade her not to go back to school, to have another baby instead, she thought what she overheard must have been true. That made her really angry, and that's why she went ahead and applied and got a grant and started summer school.''

Jack lifted his head, and with one finger he turned Gracie's chin toward him. ''Okay, but how has that changed now?''

Gracie smiled at him as though he'd just won an award. ''Good question. The answer is that at the first counseling session, Troy said something about his grandmother, and Annie confronted him with what she'd overheard.''

''Oh, that doesn't sound like a good thing.'' Jack shook his head.

''But it was! Troy was able to convince her that just because his grandmother said it was true, didn't make it true.''

''Ah.'' Losing interest in Annie and Troy, Jack ran

his fingers into the hair above Gracie's ear, feeling its silky texture.

She punched his chest, gaining his immediate attention. "Okay, that's enough about my sister and her family for tonight. I'll shut up."

"Gracie, I'm glad they're working things out. Austin and Andy need both parents." He bent down and kissed her.

For a few moments, he lost himself in the rush of sensation that flowed through him, sensitizing him to everything about Gracie.

Finally, she pulled away. "I should go in."

"Now?" he asked.

She chuckled. "Yes, now. We have work to do tomorrow, remember? Vacation's over."

He exhaled. "Yeah."

"You're spending the day in Oak Park?" She pushed the door open.

"Right. I'm meeting with the new client." He took a step backward, though everything inside him yearned to stay with her.

"Are you sure you don't need me?" She paused in the doorway.

Yes, I need you. I'll always need you. "I'll be fine on my own." Then he held up one hand as though taking an oath. "I promise that I'll be on my best customer-oriented behavior. And I'll pick you up here at six to take you to dinner."

"Good." She stepped all the way inside and paused again.

"Good night," he said, not moving.

"Good night." She stared at him and then slowly shut the door. The lock clicked.

Jack walked out to his car and climbed in. The night was warm but not sultry. A cool breeze was now whiffling the leaves overhead. He didn't feel like going home. Why not just spend a few hours at the office? He had some files on hard disks left from Tom that he wanted to scan to see if he should save the data or delete it.

An hour later, Jack was staring at the screen of his computer in the quiet storefront office. What he saw there angered him beyond belief.

How could Tom have betrayed him like that!

Chapter Thirteen

The following evening in a chic and very cosmopolitan restaurant, Gracie sat on the edge of her chair beside Jack and across from Cliff and his fiancée, hoping she was wrong.

"I'm glad we made reservations." Cliff glanced around the crowded dining room, agleam with lustrous white table linen and gilded silverware. "I thought business would be thin with everyone out of town on vacation, but I was wrong."

Sitting very straight on her cushioned red velvet seat, Gracie sensed undeniable but unseen tension radiating from Jack. She'd felt it in the car when he picked her up. But he'd merely passed off her questions and talked nonstop computerese about what he'd done all day on their new account in Oak Park.

Jack talking a lot and only in technical language was always a bad sign.

Dear Lord, I sense a change in him from only last night. What's happened to make him so resentful again?

Beside Jack's dad, Gloria, Cliff's slender fiancée, looked too young to be a grandmother. She had a golf-and-tennis tan. Her shoulder-length graying hair was highlighted blond and pulled back severely into a clip at her nape. Her linen pantsuit probably had all the right labels and she wore a chunky matching bracelet and earrings set that looked to be eighteen-carat gold.

By contrast, Gracie felt that the strand of pearls she had inherited from her mother and her new summer dress of pale-yellow cotton with white buttons and belt screamed "discount store!"

Cliff wore a well-tailored sport jacket. But Jack hadn't changed from his work clothes, a pair of chinos and a casual knit shirt. That should have been her first warning. *I should have insisted he change or refused to come along. This is going to be bad.* She nearly buried her head in her hands.

"Well, it's nice to meet you at last, Jack," Gloria said, when the two couples were suddenly alone after the waiter seated them.

"Nice?" Jack crooked an eyebrow. "Maybe 'astonishing' would be a better word. My dad and I hadn't spoken in years, until a few months ago."

Jack's tone of voice was just this side of offensive.

Gracie endured its aftermath, the awkward silence at their table that ensued while ice clinked in glasses and well-bred conversation hummed all around them.

When no one broke the intimidating hush, Gracie took a bracing sip of ice water and made herself ask, "Gloria, how did you and Cliff meet?"

"We met at a charity fund-raiser." Gloria glanced at Cliff at her side, her affection showing in the way she smiled at him and reached for his hand. "I'm very much involved in the search for a cure for type I diabetes."

"Yeah, my dad goes in for that charity stuff. Good public relations." Jack tossed this verbal grenade in a too-casual tone and leaned back in his chair, staring down his nose at his dad.

Gracie had the urge to drag Jack aside and tell him to knock it off. Instead, she ignored him as the others were doing and smiled.

"Type I? That's the type that children get, isn't it?"

"Yes, it is." Cliff's steely tone showed how he was taking Jack's behavior—not well. "Gloria's second daughter was diagnosed when she was only eight."

Jack said nothing, just sat with his arms crossed.

"I'm sorry to hear that. Type I is the one treated with injections, right?" Gracie's new white pumps were pinching her toes, but she didn't dare slip them off under the table. She had to be ready for a quick exit. *Don't push your luck, Jack, please.*

"Yes," Gloria continued, "I can't tell you what a shock it was to me to have it happen, though my husband had an older sister who died in childhood." Looking down, Gloria swirled the water in her glass, making the ice *chink-chink.* "She had diabetes, but her family didn't recognize the symptoms and they lost her to a diabetic coma back in the late 1950s."

"How sad." Gracie leaned forward, drawn by sympathy to Gloria.

"Yes, it was." Gloria moved her focus to Gracie. "And since it can be hereditary, Ted and I watched our children for the symptoms. Unfortunately, our Debbie was the one who got the wrong gene."

"I've heard that they are making all kinds of advances in research," Jack said, finally breaking his deafening silence.

Gracie felt a rush of relief. Maybe Jack would calm down now. She chanced a look at him, but saw only his profile.

"My mom, you know, has rheumatoid arthritis, another hereditary disease," Jack commented.

"Yes," Gloria smiled a real, not just a polite smile. "She seemed like a lovely person when I met her."

"She mentioned she'd met you." Jack hunched forward as though ready to throw a punch.

Gracie moved forward on her chair, ready to put her hand over his mouth—anything to stop him from launching another attack.

But Jack opened his mouth and let the poison flow.

"You noticed that my mom's still living in the run-down little house she was left with *after* my dad dumped her. Now she's having to spend a lot of her limited funds for remodeling. If my dad's *second* wife hadn't bled him nearly dry after their divorce, maybe my mom's standard of living wouldn't have suffered quite so much—"

"That's enough, Jack." Cliff slid forward also. "I've made mistakes in my life and I've paid for them. Unfortunately, you and your mother also paid. For that, I'm deeply sorry."

Jack tried to respond.

Cliff raised his voice, talking over Jack, "But if you've only come tonight to make my future wife miserable, I won't let this dinner continue. I may deserve your spite, but she does not."

Feeling as though every eye were upon them, Gracie wanted to slink under the white linen tablecloth.

Jack rose, almost knocking over his chair. "You're right. I'm sorry, Gloria. I have nothing against you except your taste in men. Come on, Gracie, we're leaving."

She wanted to remonstrate with him, but not in this public place. She rose with as much dignity as she could muster. "Thanks for the invitation, Cliff." She shook his hand and then his fiancée's. "And, Gloria, it was very nice to meet you. I wish you and Cliff all the best."

Jack had already turned and was stalking away.

Gracie followed him grimly, her face flaming with an embarrassment she'd done nothing to deserve.

What caused this, Lord? What do I say to him?

Standing stiffly out front beside Jack, she wouldn't look at him while they waited for the valet to bring up their car. She maintained her dignified silence as Jack seated her and then went around to the driver's side.

Their furious silence continued until they left downtown far behind them, since Gracie didn't trust herself to speak and feared distracting Jack in heavy city traffic.

Finally, Jack muttered, "Sorry, I didn't intend to make you feel bad."

"How very inadequate, *Jack.*" Gracie couldn't remember ever feeling so angry that her words burned fiery-hot as they passed over her tongue. "If you didn't want to meet her, why didn't you just cancel the dinner?" She glared at him.

"He's a manipulator, a controller." Jack didn't sound as though he had even heard her. "I can't stand that. And I won't be manipulated."

"How has he manipulated you?" Gracie threw her hands upward. "I can't understand you. Yesterday, you were fine. What happened in the past twenty-four hours to make you act like this?"

Jack clamped his mouth shut. A sleek black sports car cut in front of them and Jack punched his horn.

"You've just fulfilled a contract with his medical Board. That's all. How did Cliff manipulate you?"

Gracie heard the noise of a train rattling in the distance.

"I don't want to talk about it." He sped through a yellow light that turned red just as he entered the intersection.

"Watch your driving." Gracie glanced around for any police cars. "You'll get a ticket, Jack."

"I'm fine," he snapped.

"No, you're not. And you're not talking sense. I thought you'd made progress since the beginning of summer."

"I don't want to talk about it," Jack repeated, tailgating an orange delivery truck in front of them.

She knew what he was talking about, but exasperation flamed in the pit of her stomach, too. "Fine. Please take me home."

"I promised you dinner." Leaving only inches to spare, he surged past the truck and whipped back into the right lane. "We could stop and pick up something—"

"I have no appetite," Gracie snapped. Jack never drove aggressively like this! "I can't eat when I'm this upset. Please slow down, Jack."

"I'm sorry. I didn't mean to upset *you*," Jack said, his voice dipping lower, sounding sorry for the first time that evening. He slowed, no longer riding the bumper in front of them.

"Don't you realize that when you hurt someone, you damage yourself as well?" Gracie turned to glare at him. "I know you profess to be a Christian, but I fail to see any of that in you tonight. Why can't you see that this antagonism toward your father is eating up your life?"

"It's not eating up my life. I have a great life—"

"You spend your life with your head stuck inside a computer, just like Mrs. Groshky said!" The words burst loud and harsh from Gracie. "You hide from life. You hide from me!"

A moment of hostile silence passed. With relief, Gracie watched her neighborhood come into view—people sitting on their porches and children in bright summer shorts and tops playing in the park across from the church.

"You don't understand," Jack said, defending himself. "You've never been hurt, humiliated. *You've* never been…left behind. Mike never made *your* mom cry."

"I don't have to have suffered the way you did," she retorted, "in order to know what's good for you."

Gracie turned to face him, the seat belt restraining her. "If you let your anger and hurt from your father's errors linger year after year—then he *is* manipulating you, controlling you. Not because of anything he is doing, but because of what you are doing to yourself. Let it go. Cliff made a mistake. He admits he did wrong and wants to start over. Let him. Start a new relationship with him. Please. For your own sake."

"I can't."

"You mean you won't even try." Gracie swung away from him, hiding sudden tears.

"I can't." The brittle words sounded as though they came from deep in Jack's soul.

"Then, at least tell me what triggered this. Why did this evening turn out this way?"

Reaching Gracie's alley garage, Jack parked and turned off the ignition. He propped his hands against the steering wheel and stared straight ahead.

"Tell me, Jack. After what you put me through tonight at that restaurant, I have a right to know."

Silence. Gracie rolled down her window and the hot, moist summer breeze wafted inside the air-conditioned car along with the voices of children playing. She waited, still wiping away a few warm tears.

"I didn't go home right away last night." Jack finally began to let hard-fought words come. "I decided to go through some old files and disks leftover from Tom and weed out the stuff we didn't need. I found an old disk that had some information about how Tom got together the capital for LIT's launch."

"What did you find?" Gracie wouldn't look at him. She stared at the golden fingers of dusk, interlacing the tall green maples high above the rooftops.

"I found a list of the investors—and one of them was Cliff Lassater." Jack's tone turned acid. "Tom knew I didn't want any start-up money from my dad and he took it anyway and hid it from me!"

Gracie closed her eyes. *Why now, Lord? Why did*

he have to find that just when we'd finally made pro-
gress? I don't understand. Help me help him. "That
was wrong of Tom, but why does that disturb you
now? That happened years ago."

"Don't you get it?" Jack nearly shouted. "It's
always about him, about how he looks to others!
He's trying to buy his way back into my life—maybe
to impress Gloria. He's trying to win me over, put
on a good act. It won't work."

"That doesn't jibe with the facts. All Cliff has
done is hire you to do a job for his Board and try to
introduce you to his fiancée. That's all, Jack."

"You don't get it—"

"You're right!" Gracie couldn't keep her voice
down. "I don't get why you're letting something that
happened years ago still make you miserable."

"Because he hasn't changed!" Jack roared. "He
showed the kind of man he was the day he walked
out on my mom—"

"You're wrong. *I* get it, Jack. You don't." Gracie
got out of the car, slammed the door and hurried
through the chain-link gate into her backyard. It
clanged shut behind her. Gracie felt the sound, almost an echo of the door shutting in her heart.

Why did I ever think I could make a difference in
him? Why did I think he could forget the past and
have a future with me? If he can't forgive, he'll never
be able to open up his heart to me.

"Jack, this is your mother."
The next day, Jack squinted at the clock. It was

only six-thirty in the morning. "Mom?" He yawned into the phone and then a thought nudged him awake. "Is there something wrong?"

"I want to see you today."

His mom sounded funny—stern and mad like she had when he stayed out after curfew in high school. "What?"

"Are you working today?" she barked.

"Yes, I have to go to Oak Park—"

"Come here as soon as you finish your day there."

Jack fumed. "Mom, did Dad call you about last night?"

"No, your father didn't."

The phone line clicked.

He stared at the phone.

Chapter Fourteen

Outside his mother's back door, Jack heard the *rrr-ing buzz* as the air conditioner turned on. Heat from the black asphalt drive made his feet burn inside his shoes. Still, Jack hesitated. For the first time that he could recall, he didn't want to open this door.

What did his mom want? Everything that had happened the night before, especially the way Gracie had gotten out of his car and fled from him, rolled through him like a very efficient steamroller. What now?

His stomach churning, he marched inside. "Mom? It's me, Jack!" He bounded up the three steps into the kitchen.

His mother looked over her shoulder from the sink where she was washing supper dishes. "Are you hungry?"

Ready for whatever came, this everyday greeting was a letdown. "No."

"Did you eat?" Her voice went on just like always, not the way it had sounded on the phone this morning.

"No, I'm not hungry." *What do you want from me?*

She frowned at him and then turned to her chore again. "Cold chicken in the fridge."

He wanted to argue that he wasn't hungry, but the scent of fried chicken in the kitchen made his stomach growl…loudly. He hadn't taken time to eat.

After washing his hands at the sink, he got out the plastic-wrapped plate of chicken and sat down at the table.

His mother poured him a glass of iced tea and set it down in front of him. Then she returned to the sink.

"Mike was here for supper."

"Okay." Jack pulled out a golden drumstick and took a bite. Was this about Mike?

"He phoned me at six this morning and told me that you upset Gracie last night."

Oh. Jack chewed, but the juicy meat suddenly lost its flavor. "I didn't mean to."

"I don't want you to get the wrong idea. Gracie didn't tell him what you'd said or done to upset her. But he knew that the two of you had gone to have dinner with Cliff and Gloria—"

"Mike should mind his own business," Jack muttered. He tossed the drumstick back onto the plate.

"Gracie is Mike's business. Just as you are my business."

His mother's sharp tone made him sit up and stare at her back.

"I'm afraid I haven't taken care of my business as I should have either." Mom shut off the water and dried her hands on the faded apron tied around the waist of her jean shorts.

"What are you talking about?"

Mom still faced the sink. "I've shielded myself from telling you the truth. I've always told myself it was better for you if you didn't know. But now I think it's time you knew the truth."

"The truth?" Jack wiped his fingers on a paper napkin and tossed it on the table.

His mom didn't move, didn't turn toward him. She seemed to shrink into herself. "I'm so sorry to have to tell you this, but I think you need to know it so you can understand your father better."

Jack didn't like the way this sounded. "Mom, I—"

"Your father and I had to get married. I was three months pregnant with you when we married."

His mother's stark words paralyzed him.

"We weren't in love." She sounded as though she were reading out of a book. "We'd only dated casually. We were in college. Neither of us was religious then and the sexual revolution was happening.''

Jack couldn't say a word.

"I didn't want to have an abortion." The matter-of-fact recital continued. "The women in my family aren't very fertile. I was an only child of an only child. I was afraid that you might be the only baby I'd ever have. And as it turned out, I was right." She brushed this aside. "Anyway, I told Cliff, but I didn't expect him to marry me. We weren't in love, but I thought he should know."

Jack's heart pounded and his ears buzzed.

"Cliff insisted that we marry. He said he wanted to be a part of his child's life. His parents had divorced when he was little and he'd never seen his dad except for a couple of weeks each summer. He said they were always polite strangers to each other."

Jack closed his eyes. His mother's voice had softened now. He could hear the pain there, and also the sympathy for his dad.

"So we got married." She finally turned away from the sink and faced him. "And you were born. I thought we did pretty well. I worked. Cliff continued pre-med and helped out with child care—watching you when I worked evenings. He loved you, Jack. He still does."

"Then, why did he leave us?" His own pained words shocked Jack. He hadn't meant to speak them.

"He didn't leave *you*, Jack. He left *me*. And I didn't blame him." His mother turned from the sink and sat down across from him. "Don't you see? How could I try to hold on to him when he'd only married me because of you? We were good friends. We both loved you, but in the end, that wasn't enough for him. And unfortunately, someone took advantage of those feelings. Our marriage ended and he walked right into a very bad second marriage. I felt responsible for that, too."

Jack felt tears sting his eyes. He blinked them away.

"This is a lot to dump on you. But it's time you knew the truth. I don't want my mistakes to mess up what's been happening between you and Gracie this summer. Do you know how long I've hoped that you would wake up and notice how much in love she is with you?"

Jack stared at his mom. "Gracie...in love with me?"

Mom shook her head at him. "She's good at hiding it from you, but I noticed it right away, and so did Tom, I think. She's so good for you, Jack, so down-to-earth and she has such a big heart. She would make a lovely mother. An excellent wife, too."

Jack's insides felt like a dozen yo-yo's being spun up and down and in and out. "Mom, I..."

She reached and pulled over a hand-size photo album he hadn't noticed before. "Here. I was looking at this today, remembering. I want you to look through the photos and tell me that your dad didn't love you—and then, try to make me believe it.'' She opened the album and pushed it toward him.

Glancing down, he saw a photo of his dad holding him as a baby. His father was beaming with obvious pride.

His mother stabbed the air in front of Jack's nose with her index finger. ''You are the one who's pushed your father away. Cliff deeply regrets hurting you and was humiliated over his marriage to that woman. But in Gloria, I think he's finally found someone he can spend the rest of his life with happily.

''Maybe, if I had been a Christian when he wanted to leave,'' she continued, ''I would have fought harder and longer to keep him. Maybe we could even have managed to stay married. But I didn't. I hated the divorce and how it hurt you. But a decade has passed. God can forgive us, your father and me. Why can't you, Jack?''

Jack stared down at the photos of his father and him. He flipped the page to one of his dad helping him walk.

''And I know you want to pay for the remodeling—'' His mom sounded like she was slowing down, nearing the end. ''But Cliff has already insisted on taking care of it for me. I've accepted his offer and will pay off the home equity loan I'd taken out. But I intend to repay him the principal over the next few years, even though he insists it isn't necessary. Oh, and I might as well tell you that Mike proposed to me last night.''

Jack stared at his mother. It felt as if she'd hit him with a one-two punch.

"Life goes on. Mike, Cliff, Gloria and I are going on. Don't get stuck in the past, Jack. Don't mess things up with Gracie.'' She got up and went back to the sink.

He heard water running and then the sounds of his mother drying and putting away dishes and silverware. But he felt removed from her. The yo-yo's inside him slowed but did not stop. *What just happened here, Lord? I can't process it all.*

He rose and started toward the door. "'Bye, Mom. I…''

She came to him at the head of the back steps and hugged him. "Call me tomorrow, okay?''

He nodded and headed out. He got into his car and started driving. He went over and over what his mom had revealed. He barely paid attention to where he was driving. He just couldn't stop. A restlessness pushed him on and on, up street after street. Twilight glowed and dimmed. Night fell. Finally, he knew where he had to go.

Minutes later, he stood at Gracie's back door and knocked. A sense of urgency bubbled in him. Gracie would know what all this meant. She would put it all in place for him.

Gracie opened the door and his heart turned over

when he saw her troubled expression. "What's wrong?" he asked.

"Nothing." She stood at the door but did not welcome him in.

"You look sad." He had to hold his arms down to keep from drawing her to him. *I didn't want to make you sad.*

"What do you want, Jack? It's late." She looked down, not meeting his eyes. She wore a pair of cut-offs and a tank top, just as she had at the cabin.

"I need to talk to you." *Hold you like I did at the lake.*

"About?" she asked in a drill-sergeant tone.

"My mom and my dad." Jack edged a step closer to the door, to Gracie.

With a long, very intense look, she held him at bay. "Your mom and *your* dad, not my dad?"

He thought that over. "Right."

She stepped back. "Okay, come in." Without a backward glance, she led him to the cozy living room and sank onto the couch. "Sit."

Still standing, he couldn't stop gazing at her—so petite and pale—against the blue and white sofa with yellow throw pillows. She folded her shapely legs under her as though shielding herself from him.

Don't hide from me, Gracie. I need you to put everything together for me. So I will understand it. He forced himself to keep his distance, but the memory of kissing Gracie filled him with a hopeless anguish.

He finally eased down onto the edge of a chair across from her. She watched him as though he might sprout a third eye. Even that first time he'd come here in May and she'd been so upset about her sister leaving, Gracie had been more welcoming. *This is my fault. I made my parents unhappy and I've made Gracie unhappy.*

"What can I do for you?" she asked him.

He stared at her, trying to figure out how to open up, how to begin. *I can't. I can't tell her.*

His cell phone rang in his pocket. He took it out. "Yes?"

"Jack, I need you to come right away to the main Hope financial office," Cliff said, his words rapid-fire. "I got a call that some files have been tampered with—"

Not now. "Did anyone touch them?"

"No, I'm here to make sure no one does. Can you come right—"

"I'll be there as fast as I can." Jack snapped the phone shut. "I'll be back. My dad needs me at Hope."

Chapter Fifteen

A head in the low light, Cliff stood guard over the computers at Hope's main financial office. The cubicles were silent and the night showed dark at each large plate-glass window.

Jack hurried through the glass door into the room, his eyes going to the bright computer monitor. He looked to his dad, recalling their recent parting, and didn't know what to say.

"I made sure no one messed with the files." Cliff's voice was gruff and he looked grim.

"Good...thanks." Jack took cover in his role as computer expert. Would he finally get a clue to the hacker's identity and finish this job for good? He sat down at the monitor and began tapping keys.

"Someone was working late, noticed that some files had just been changed and called me. I told them, 'Don't touch anything,' and then I headed straight here and called you right away."

"You did just what you should have." Jack accessed the file that showed the system activity—who had been in and out of the files that day.

"Will you be able to get him?" Cliff leaned over Jack, also reading the computer monitor.

"I don't know. It depends on how good…" Jack fell silent as a window opened on the screen and showed someone in the act of accessing files.

Jack shoved the chair back and flipped through a notebook of passwords he'd brought with him. He watched the files being altered right in front of his eyes. "It's happening," he breathed. "The hacker is doing his thing right now."

"What?" Cliff sounded shocked and bent farther to view the monitor.

"And now I know who it is. It's a Board member."

"Collins?"

"No." Jack showed his dad the page with his thumb by the entry and the password, and then got to his feet. "I'm going to catch him red-handed." Jack charged out of the room.

Cliff raced after him, shouting questions.

Jack ignored them. It was good to have Cliff along as a witness. But after last night, he'd have chosen almost anyone else.

Within half an hour, Jack had driven out to the

suburbs and up to an imposing home on a quiet street in an exclusive subdivision. He'd been there before.

"I can't believe this is true," Cliff said again. "You've got something wrong."

Cliff had questioned him over and over on the trip. Jack had ignored most of the questions. Why talk? He was right and he could prove it.

"I'm going in." Jack opened his car door and got out. He confronted his dad. "I didn't get it wrong. You saw someone at this house use Dunn's password while we were at the main computer. Whoever it is began altering numbers in accounts without permission."

His father tried to interrupt.

Jack refused to be stopped. "This hacker has done everything but mess with patients' medical records. That could cost people pain and maybe even their lives. Are you coming or am I going in alone?"

Without a word, Cliff got out and kept up with Jack as they raced up the drive to the front door.

Jack rang the doorbell.

Two minutes passed by his watch.

He rang the bell again.

A muffled, irritated-sounding shout came from inside.

The door swung open and Dunn in pajamas glared at Jack. "What the heck are you two doing ringing my doorbell at this hour—"

Jack shoved past Dunn and looked around the dimly lit house. "Where's your computer?"

"What?" Dunn gawked at him.

"Your computer," Jack demanded. "Where is it?"

"Upstairs in my office." Dunn rubbed his forehead. "Do you have any idea what time—"

Jack ignored Dunn and darted up the staircase.

"Hey! My wife's up there!" Dunn chased after Jack. "We're all in bed for the night. Hold up."

Jack topped the stairs.

"Stop!" Dunn roared.

Jack glimpsed the light under the first door at the top of the landing go out.

Mrs. Dunn, fastening a pale shiny robe around her slim form, met Jack in the upper hall. "What are you doing here?"

"What's in that room?" Jack pointed to the closed room, which had suddenly gone dark.

"That's my son's room—" Dunn came up behind Jack. "I'm going to have to ask you to leave."

"Dunn, it's about the hacker." Cliff appeared at the top of the staircase, too.

Jack stepped forward. He twisted the doorknob and thrust open the door.

Sitting at a computer desk, Dunn's preteen son glared at Jack by the light cast by the glowing monitor. "Hey, this is *my* room!"

Jack strode in and flipped on the wall light switch. There, beside the computer, was Dunn's "token key," a small rectangle with a liquid-crystal display that cycled an endless variety of combinations of four numbers every fifteen seconds. Numbers that had to be entered along with the password to gain access to Hope files.

Jack grabbed up the token key and swung around to Dunn. "Why did you give this to your son?" He shook the key in front of Dunn's face. "You knew it was to be used by you alone."

Dunn gaped at Jack.

Mrs. Dunn and Cliff clustered behind Dunn in the doorway.

"Well?" Jack prompted.

"I didn't give it—" Dunn began.

"I took it!" The son's jaw jutted belligerently. "I'm the hacker." The boy barked a dry, cheerless laugh. "Took you long enough to find me, big shot."

Jack heard Mrs. Dunn gasp.

"Damon, no!" she exclaimed. "You're making that up."

"No, I'm not! *I* did it." The thin kid with spiked hair wearing summer pajamas folded his arms over his thin chest. "Dad says I can't do anything—"

"Stop lying, Damon," his mother pleaded. "They might believe you."

"Listen to your mother, boy." Dunn shouldered past Jack. "You, the hacker? Make me laugh. You couldn't do it. You don't have the brains. You—"

"Just because I don't get good grades, doesn't mean I'm dumb," Damon retorted. "I outsmarted Mr. Computer Nerd here!"

"Yeah, right," Dunn sneered. "You outsmarted

our very experienced, very expensive computer expert—"

"I started by adding zeros—'cause you said I was just a zero." The son's tone matched the father's, dripping sarcasm and disrespect. "Then, 'cause you're so cheap, I decided to give everyone raises—"

"Dunn," Jack cut in, "now that I know where the attack came from, I can trace your computer and prove it was the one used in compromising the Hope system. But I don't have to. He's got your token key in hand. That's proof enough."

Everyone fell silent—the four of them standing around the boy at the computer desk. In the leaden silence, Jack heard the air conditioner whine as it cycled on.

Then Mrs. Dunn began to sob. "I told you to spend more time with Damon. I told you something was going on with him. Why don't you listen to me?"

Dunn rounded on her. "I have work to do. He's past the age where I should have to be around holding his hand. You want me to bring home the big bucks? Well, I have to work long hours to do that."

"Who wants you around more anyway?" Damon sneered.

Jack eased backward. Solving the mystery had excited him. But he hadn't considered the effect of his unmasking the Dunns' son as the hacker.

"I don't need you here—" Damon's voice rose as

he verbally attacked his father ''—watching me, telling me what to do. I don't need you.''

This last sentence—so bitter, so acidic—echoed through Jack. His memory summoned up a scene. He was standing outside his mother's back door, shouting at his dad, *''Go on and leave. I don't need you!''*

His heart raced, making him a little nauseated. He glanced over his shoulder at his dad. *I don't want to see myself in this situation. This has nothing to do with me and my dad.*

Cliff's face looked frozen in a deep frown. He motioned for Jack to fall back.

Jack obeyed, leaving the mother, father and son alone in the room.

What would happen now? The kid was a minor, but he'd broken laws, caused all kinds of expense—stuff the kid hadn't even considered. He'd just tried to get his dad's attention. In the worst possible way.

With a hand on Jack's sleeve, Cliff led him farther down the hall. ''I think we should leave.''

Jack didn't know what was best to do and really, the present dilemma wasn't occupying him.

In the dark hall, recollection after recollection poured through his mind—scenes of Cliff slowly, painfully moving away from him when he was in high school, basketball games Cliff never showed up for, the evenings Jack had shot baskets alone in the drive while his dad worked late.

And then scenes where Jack rejected his dad. The anguish and anger roiled back as potent as they had been years before, now rubbing Jack raw inside. "Okay," he managed to mumble.

They shuffled down the stairs side by side and quietly let themselves out. Without exchanging a word, they got back into the car and Jack drove off.

The silence lasted until Jack pulled up in front of the Hope financial offices building.

Jack kept his eyes forward, looking at the pattern of lights on the building. No words came to him except the ones he didn't want to say.

Silence.

"I know we had to find out who was doing this," Cliff finally said. "It was too serious to ignore, but I feel awful for the Dunns."

Jack nodded, his tortured stomach doing a free fall.

"Well, I guess I'll get home." Cliff reached for the door handle.

"Dad—" Gripping the steering wheel, Jack turned to him. "I'm sorry…"

In the glow of the nearby streetlight, Cliff froze, looking back at Jack. Finally, he asked, "You mean about how you treated Gloria?"

"Yes." *And for a lot more.* "It won't happen again." Jack felt a little sick, as though he'd been running and was dehydrated. "I'd like to make it up to her…and you."

A pause.

"Good." Cliff cleared his throat. "Good. I'd like that, so would Gloria."

Able to loosen his hold on the wheel, Jack offered Dad his hand. "Thanks."

Cliff accepted his hand and shook it. "Good."

Healing flowed through Jack, warm and freeing. He took a deep breath.

Then Cliff closed the door. Through the open window, he said, "Call me and we'll make another date."

"I will." Jack's pulse still pounded in the aftermath of this exchange.

"Good night, Son."

"Good night, Dad."

Jack drove straight to Gracie's house and parked in the alley by Mike's garage.

Her neighborhood was quiet and dark, but Jack had to speak to Gracie. Make things right.

Getting out, he recalled their parting conversation last night. "You don't get it, Jack," Gracie had said. *Lord, I get it now. Help me prove that to Gracie.*

I love her.

He ran to her back door and knocked—hard. He waited. Mosquitoes buzzed his ear and he swatted them away. Finally, the back light was switched on and Gracie drew aside the little curtain to peer at him through the high back door window.

She unlocked the door and opened it a wedge. "It's after midnight," she whispered in a what-are-you-nuts? tone. "What do you—"

"I caught the hacker."

She opened the door and let him in. She was dressed in rumpled shorts and T-shirt.

Her hair was tousled and Jack had the undeniable urge to kiss her. He pulled her to him, pressing his face next to hers. "Forgive me, Gracie." He kissed her.

For a moment, she relaxed against him, joining in the kiss. Then abruptly, she pushed him away. "Why are you kissing me?"

He let her go. "I was wrong." He raked his hands through his hair. "But I finally got it tonight."

"Got it? Got what?"

"Remember? Last night you said I didn't get it but you did. Tonight, I got it."

She motioned him toward the worn wicker furniture on the screened-in back porch. She sat down on a porch swing. "Start at the beginning. Where did you go tonight when you left me? You said—"

"My dad had been called about something happening to the files at the Hope financial center." Jack sank down beside her. The swing swayed under him. He fought the urge to forgo explanations and just kiss her again. Sitting on the unstable swing reminded him just how he felt about persuading Gracie to love him.

"What did Cliff want?"

"Cliff called me and then stood guard so no one would tamper with them."

She nodded. "Go on."

Gracie, can't we stop talking? I want to kiss you

again. "Anyway, while we were looking at the files," Jack explained, trying to get it over with, "I saw the hacker enter the system and I immediately saw the password he used."

She drew in breath. "Who was it?"

Gracie, just let me hold you. "It was Dunn's password. Remember him? We went to his pool party."

"Yes, but Dr. Dunn? I don't get it."

"My dad and I took off for his place—"

"Why would Dr. Dunn tamper with files?" she interrupted.

He rushed to clarify. "It wasn't Dunn. I found his son using his token key."

"His son? How awful." Gracie's voice sank.

Her instant sympathy moved him and he sat closer to her. The swing shifted under him again. "It was bad. The kid…name's Damon…said he did it to show his dad he was smart, even if he didn't get good grades. It was an ugly scene. Everyone was mad, but I saw it all…finally."

"What did you see, Jack?" Gracie leaned toward him, her head cocked.

"I saw myself in that kid. He was willing to cause all kinds of chaos—just because he was angry with his dad."

"Well, after meeting Dr. Dunn," she said, "I can imagine the kind of father he is."

"Yeah, the kid was so resentful, so angry."

Silence.

"Gracie, when we talked last night, you wanted

me to make up with my dad. When I went there
tonight…'' He looked to her. *Help me put it into
words, Gracie.*

''I understand.'' She slid forward till her knee
touched his, the swing rocking gently under them.
''You've been angry with your dad a long time. Finally, now, you saw that you were still acting like
this kid. Your dad did wrong, but that doesn't mean
it should wreck your relationship with him forever.''

''Or with you.'' He took the plunge and wrapped
his arms around her softness. He clung to her as the
swing swayed back and forth. ''You're right. I've
buried my head in my work and pushed away practically everyone else—even you.'' His mother's
words came back to him, *''Gracie's in love with
you.''*

''Do you love me, Gracie?''

She withdrew from him.

''I said that wrong, I know. Wait.'' He rolled
words around in his mind. He paused, trying to sort
out what he was feeling, thinking—groping for
words. ''I'm no good at saying things, you know
that. You always help me—''

''You have to say this, Jack. I can't say it for
you.'' She pushed against the floor with her bare foot
and the swing moved forward and back.

''Will you give us a chance?'' Jack stopped the
swing by putting his foot down. ''I've pushed everyone away because of my resentment toward my dad.

But I can't lose you, Gracie. I think I'm in love with you.''

She opened her arms.

He moved into them and rested his cheek against hers. ''Oh, Gracie.'' He drew her closer against him in rhythm with the swing.

''I never thought you'd love me,'' she whispered. ''I'm not special like Annie—''

''Don't ever say that again.'' He pulled her head back to look her directly in the eyes. ''You are the most wonderful woman in the world. And anyone who argues with that, even you, will get an argument from me.''

Her eyes filled with tears. ''Then, I know you truly love me, Jack.'' She kissed him.

He responded in kind, a long sweet exchange.

When their lips parted at last, more words, important words came to him. ''You *are* special, Gracie.'' He made the swing sway gently. ''It's not just because I love you. It's true. Just ask anyone who knows you. Gracie, you're one in a million. If you love me, I'm the luckiest man in the world.''

Gracie leaned against him, her joy flowing with sweet tears. ''I love you, Jack. Forever.''

''Forever,'' he agreed. *Lord, help me make her happy.*

Epilogue

~~~

Mike, in a black suit, and Sandy, in a silvery party dress, held hands at the front of the small chapel. The glass-covered candles at each window along the sides of the room were decorated with sprigs of holly and purple advent ribbon to reflect Christmas, only ten days away.

Only family and close friends had been invited to the intimate wedding. These included Annie and Troy, who were back together, and Gloria and Cliff, who were planning a spring wedding. Mr. Pulaski had walked the bride up the aisle. Jack stood beside Mike as his best man. Gracie, as maid of honor, held Sandy's red rose bridal bouquet.

As the minister directed the exchanging of rings, Gracie gazed across at Jack, so handsome in his black suit. Their wedding would be a winter one also. But they had put it off until Valentine's Day.

As she heard her dad say "With this ring, I thee wed," her heart swelled with love for him, for Sandy, for her mother who must be smiling down on them from heaven, and for Jack. *My beloved*.

Tears misted Gracie's eyes.

Then footsteps pattered up behind her. She glanced down to see Austin and Andy, in their first suits, pushing in front.

"We wanna see the rings," Austin said in a quiet, awed voice.

"Yeah," Andy agreed, "everybody's in our way."

Muted chuckles rippled through the wedding guests. Gracie heard Annie moan with embarrassment. But Mike and Sandy showed the boys the rings. Then Jack reached for the boys and pulled them to stand by him.

He would never make the mistakes that Cliff and Dr. Dunn had with their sons. Jack stroked Andy's blond hair and laid a hand on Austin's shoulder.

Gracie's heart turned over. *Thank you, Father. All good gifts do come from above.*

*   *   *   *   *

Look for Cousin Patience's story,
TESTING HIS PATIENCE,
coming out June 2004,
only from Lyn Cote and Love Inspired,
as the SISTERS OF THE HEART
continues…

Dear Reader,

Thanks for taking the time to get to know Gracie and Jack. Do you know a couple like them? I do. In fact, my husband and I are the prototypes for the well-organized take-charge woman and the quiet man who thinks in numbers. No one would have put us together, and we have celebrated over twenty-five years together.

I named Gracie after the late Gracie Allen, George Burns's comedienne wife. I thought it would be funny to name no-nonsense Gracie Petrov after flighty Gracie Allen. Do you remember George telling her at the end of a flight of fancy about her crazy family, "Say good-night, Gracie"? And she did it with a smile. They seemed like a couple very much in love.

The next book in this SISTERS OF THE HEART series will take Patience Andrews, Gracie's cousin, to her new teaching job in downstate Illinois. If just teaching school were all she had to do, she'd be fine. But a month into the school year, Patience will be called to jury duty and run up against the local district attorney. What will he say when he finds out she's the one responsible for his hung jury? Look for Patience's story, *Testing His Patience,* in June 2004.

Please write me at P.O. Box 864, Woodruff, WI 54568, www.booksbylyncote.com.

Best,

Lyn Cote

HEART
AND SOUL

BY

JILLIAN
HART

Taking in an injured stranger wasn't something
Michelle McKaslin would normally do, but she'd
sensed something special about Gabe Brody. But
would her heaven-sent feelings remain when she
learned who he really was—the undercover agent
investigating her family?

Don't miss

HEART AND SOUL
On sale May 2004.

Available at your favorite retail outlet.

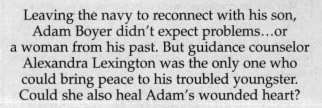

ABIDING LOVE

BY

KATE WELSH

Leaving the navy to reconnect with his son,
Adam Boyer didn't expect problems…or
a woman from his past. But guidance counselor
Alexandra Lexington was the only one who
could bring peace to his troubled youngster.
Could she also heal Adam's wounded heart?

Don't miss

ABIDING LOVE

On sale May 2004.

Available at your favorite retail outlet.

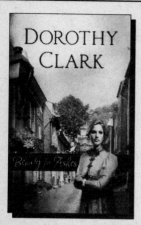

Steeple Hill Books brings you a sweeping historical saga of faith, forgiveness and loving by

DOROTHY CLARK

Available June 2004.

Save $1.00 off the purchase price of *Beauty for Ashes*.

Redeemable at participating retailers in Canada only. May not be combined with other coupons or offers.

Steeple Hill®

```
52605707
```

Visit us at www.steeplehill.com

SDC515CAN

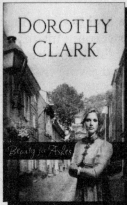

Steeple Hill Books brings you a sweeping historical saga of faith, forgiveness and loving by

DOROTHY CLARK

Available June 2004.

Save $1.00 off
the purchase price
of *Beauty for Ashes*.

**Redeemable at participating retailers in the U.S. only.
May not be combined with other coupons or offers.**

Steeple
Hill®

```
5 65373 00076 2   (8100) 0 11121
```

Visit us at www.steeplehill.com